BETTER GNOMES & GARDENS

A MYSTY HAVEN MYSTERY

Book 1

CASEY CARDEL

MP
MENTHA PRESS

MENTHA PRESS
P.O. BOX 34
WISCONSIN, USA

ISBN_13: 978-1-937629-64-9(Hard Cover)
ISBN_13: 978-1-937629-62-5(Trade Paperback)
ISBN_13: 978-1-937629-63-2(e-Book)

Library of Congress Control Number: 2022942148
BETTER GNOMES & GARDENS

Edited by: Carol Gaskins, ***Editorial Alchemy***

Printed in U.S.A

Praise
for
Better Gnomes & Gardens

"...a delightful, sparkling originality to the story's setting and plot development that should especially appeal to seasoned cozy mystery readers looking for something refreshingly new, as well as paranormal readers who want a greater element of suspense." ***-D. Donovan, Senior Reviewer, Midwest Book Review***

"Casey Cardel is a great storyteller who succeeds to keep readers turning the pages. In addition to creating a beguiling setting, the author invents a world that readers find irresistible." ***-The Book Commentary***

"Cardel's thoroughly sketched characters and setting breathe further life into the effortlessly crafted plot while the engaging prose and expert inclusion of various red herrings throughout the narrative pull the reader right in. Fans of compelling paranormal mysteries won't want to miss this one. A triumph."-
Book View Review

"Fast-paced action and paranormal intrigue seep through Cardel's tantalizing debut installment in the Mysty Haven Mysteries series. Tension stays high, with nonstop twists and new revelations, and Cardel smoothly blends the sleuthing with hefty doses of humor. Readers looking for a page-turning classic mystery won't be able to resist."
-The Prairies Book Review

ONE

"You are fired."

Monday at precisely 8:05 AM, I'd heard the three little words I'd never expected nor wanted to hear from my boss. Arguing with him, or explaining the reason for my decision, only made matters worse. The vein that popped out on the side of his temple indicated that he might've been upset.

"There's no such thing as a Bigfoot! I specifically told you not to send this article to the printer. What did you do, Bob? You sent it to the printers. We get enough flak about printing fake news from the public, and now *this*?"

"Oh, come on, Tony, it's a good story, and you know it. The information I got was a first-hand sighting." I picked up the paper and pointed to my first newspaper article, "Bigfoot Sightings Confirmed in Las Vegas."

"You told me when you hired me to make this job my own," I said. "'Take the initiative,' you said. That's what I did, Tony. Eyewitness."

The moment Tony's face turned blood red should have been my clue to leave his office. But no, not Bob McLarney, the best investigative reporter in Mysty Haven. I was right, and I wasn't going to lose my job because I had uncovered the truth of all truths: Bigfoot was real.

"I gave you a chance and paid—" He inhaled a deep breath, snapped the black rim glasses from his face, and stood abruptly. Tony's green eyes went from a happy cat-eye green to a dark menacing green that pierced straight into my soul. "*Paid* for your trip to

Las Vegas to write a story on Elvis impersonators. People love Elvis."

"Yes—yes, they do. People love Bigfoot too."

"Elvis was real, Bob."

"And so is Bigfoot."

Tony's right eye twitched, not once but in a series of spasms that didn't stop. That wasn't what made me leave his office. I went because he lifted a crooked finger and thrust it towards the door.

I didn't bother cleaning out my desk because there wasn't anything valuable after one week. With my dignity intact, I waltzed out the front door with my head held high like a matador who'd won the greatest bullfight.

The job, my first since I'd graduated from college a month before, was a surprise. A Master's degree in journalism looked good on paper but didn't mean much to an employer who wanted experience. Tony gave me the chance to prove my worth by assigning me a lead story straight off the bat. My ambition led me to provide him with the best story the *Mysty Haven Weekender* ever ran—a real scoop. Within my first week!

Okay, so he disagreed with me. Now I was back to square one. Nothing a good cup of joe couldn't fix, and I knew just the place: Maddie B's, a simple, cozy little diner on the west side of town that served the best coffee I'd ever had. Maddie's stayed busy with her regular morning cuppers and some during the lunch-hour rush. The place reminded me of a time long past, with its aluminum exterior and fifties decor. Even Maddie looked as if she'd stepped right out of a Dick Tracy comic strip.

Maddie B's had become my favorite spot for coffee and catty conversation with the locals in the short week since I took the reporter job. At twenty-three years old, I considered myself a handsome and clean-cut guy, though even at my height of six-foot-four, I never once played basketball or any other sport. My interests were books, news, and food—in that order. Some people call me a nerd, and maybe I am, or I just like to keep informed on the latest discoveries.

Mythical creatures like Bigfoot, faeries, leprechauns, vampires, and werewolves had held my interest since childhood. I grew up with sound-minded parents who encouraged reading and exploring one's imagination. So it's no surprise that my imagination ran wild, then turned into a hobby, and had now led me to become an investigative reporter.

I needed a good lead on another job, and luckily I lived in a small town where everyone talked. Unfortunately, the town had only one local newspaper, and the morning cuppers had long left the café, taking any possible good leads with them.

Mysty Haven, located in the northeastern part of Wisconsin, is a quiet place, hard to find on a Google Map. In my case, it didn't even register until I was right in the village. Once I took the newspaper job, finding an apartment had been difficult. The only cheap place I could find fully furnished was a loft apartment over an empty store building in town. The rental agent stated the location was once a shoe store. That explained the leather smell. He'd also mentioned the previous tenant had left abruptly but paid the apartment and store lease three months in advance. The owner passed the free months on to me. I'd never believed in luck, but I did think that good fortune could be found in perfect timing.

Another advantage to my ideal spot was that Maddie B's Café was located only a couple of blocks away. The aroma of fresh-brewed coffee drew me like a vampire to a single drop of blood. Maddie wasn't bad on the eyes, either. She had just the right looks for a woman to make a man want to howl at the moon on a lonely night. Those deep brown eyes behind her luscious black eyelashes conveyed a sense of mystery.

It was precisely 8:35 AM, according to the red and white vintage Coca-Cola wall clock that hung on the wall behind the counter. I paused in the doorway to survey my surroundings. The existing cuppers included a tall, stocky man who sat at a quaint table to my left with his beautiful companion.

She wasn't just beautiful—she was dangerously gorgeous. Her appeal may have been the silky blonde hair that feathered lightly on her shoulders or the tailor-made, navy blue double-breasted suit she wore. Her pale, smooth skin reminded me of a porcelain doll. And that she was, a living doll who would catch any man's attention by simply walking into a room. At first glance, this woman breathed class and money. A woman of her caliber didn't look like a regular cupper, maybe an iced coffee drinker or tea sipper.

To my right, partway along the counter sat a dusty-looking elderly gentleman nursing a cup of coffee and eating some type of sugary delight. A light coating of his dust, or a yellow-grayish powder, covered his dark grey cardigan. It appeared he might have gotten into a fight with a moth or been attacked by a giant flower. I wasn't sure who had won the battle, but I would bet it wasn't him.

Behind the antique counter stood the striking ginger-haired woman who held my heart in her hand every time I caught a whiff of her steaming cups of coffee. She knew just how I liked mine, too. Fresh and hot, with a hint of cream and a sprinkle of sugar. Amazing how she could make each cup so unique, the kind of special that made me feel as if I were the most important person in the world.

"Hiya, Bob. Back so soon? Did you forget something?" Maddie made it a point to know all her customers by name and their favorite menu items. She whipped out a spoon and had the coffee ready for me before I made it to the counter.

"Thanks, Maddie," I hoisted a hip and slid onto a red leather barstool, leaving a couple of seats between Dusty and me. I didn't want any of what he had in my precious cup of joe.

"Having a rough morning?" Soothing yet compassionate, like butter spreading over toast, her voice warmed my heart to a melting point.

"Was that in today's headlines as well? Lead investigative news reporter gets fired over fact-finding evidence that Bigfoot is real?" I took a sip of coffee, savoring the aroma and flavor for a long moment before opening my eyes.

Maddie's soft, inviting smile disappeared. "I'm sorry to hear about your job. Honestly, I don't read the newspaper."

The surprise hit me like a ton of bricks. Then it occurred to me that she probably didn't need to read the newspaper.

"Of course, you probably hear enough news from your customers." I took another sip, allowing the robust flavors to awaken each of my senses. I'd never experienced coffee like at Maddie's. Simply put, it was a magical experience that I couldn't explain.

She pursed those alluring red lips together and leaned in closer. "No, that's not it at all, Bob. I don't read the newspapers because of all the fake news."

And that's when the ginger dame shattered my heart into a million pieces. The fun didn't seem like it would ever let up today. At least the coffee was still good.

Dramatically, I pressed my right hand over my heart and sighed. "Maddie, that really hurts."

"Sorry, Bob." She shot me a sly grin and lowered her eyes into what I considered a half-flirt mode. "You know, I've got just the thing to mend a broken heart. Grimm's Bakery brought over a batch of freshly baked schnecken a few minutes ago. You know the saying: 'A cinnamon roll is good for the soul?'"

I didn't, but I nodded anyway. "Sounds lovely, but I'll just sit here and wallow." I shot her a wink, followed by a casual smile as I returned to nursing my coffee, along with my feelings.

Fake news—that's what everyone called it these days.

I never reported fake news. I reported the truth, backed up by hardcore facts and evidence. Even in college I'd made it a point to uncover the truth and write the best papers. I didn't just look at the surface but dug deep in the dirt to find the real meaning of my stories. I gave readers more than just the gravy— I gave them prime beef.

At the distracting noise of chair legs scraping on the floor, Maddie's warm brown eyes trailed to the couple behind me. I glanced in the same direction to see the big guy and the high-class dame preparing to leave the table.

"Need anything else, Mr. B?"

"I'll take some of that delicious schnecken for the road, if you don't mind, Maddie." The deep, husky voice was what I expected coming from a man of his stature.

"Sure thing. I'll be right back." Maddie tapped the counter in front of me with her perfectly manicured red nails, gave me a wink, then gracefully disappeared behind two silver doors that led into the kitchen.

Minutes later, she reappeared with a white cake box and met the big guy at the register. I couldn't help but eye his beautiful companion one more time while they waited.

Mr. B—I couldn't help but wonder what the B stood for. His towering height and size could mean Big, but usually an initial stood for a last name. I made a mental note to ask Maddie. Still new to this town, I had time to get to know everyone—just not today. Today, I had to find another job.

Maddie finished ringing up Mr. B, then turned to make a fresh pot of coffee as they left. But instead of smelling coffee, a horrible odor hit my nostrils.

That smell.

The rancid funk of a thousand years wafted from the door and punched me like a knockout in a boxing match. I clutched at the counter to brace myself momentarily until the room stopped spinning. The stench was worse than something a cat would have dragged in, perhaps something that a dog might bury. I couldn't help it. I attempted to wave the odor away from my face, but it only worsened.

Even as a small child, I always had an acute sense of smell, abstruse to others and even my parents. I learned to live with it and even depend on it through many aspects of my life—although identifying the different aromas or smells and what they meant took time, practice, and understanding. Maddie didn't seem to notice the stench, and neither did Dusty, two seats away.

"What are your plans now?" Maddie's voice turned smooth and sweet like honey, which distracted me from the horrible smell.

"I guess it's back to the job market." I took a sip from the cup, breathing it in to try to overpower the corpse-odor, which seemed to be dissipating. "I do believe there is a bright side to everything," I added. "Something will come along soon."

"Of course it will, Bob. Sometimes the very thing we think is a curse is a blessing in disguise. Maybe that job wasn't where you needed to be in your life. It's a big world, and we all have a specific part. I'm positive you'll find your way."

"Thank you, Maddie. You're right; I'll find my way soon enough."

"Sure. You're a smart, hardworking, and intelligent man with a good head on his shoulders. Why, anyone should be happy to hire you," she pronounced with her hands on her hips, squaring her shoulders like she meant business.

I like a woman who's got spunk, especially one who does a superhero power pose.

"Flattery, eh? And you learned all these things about me in less than two weeks?" I chuckled and arched a brow.

"Aw, come on, Bob, you're an investigative reporter—I bet you could probably give Sherlock Holmes a run for his money."

"Gnomes?" Old Dusty perked up. "Mine's gone missing."

"No, Doug, I said Holmes." Maddie raised her voice a bit towards him, then turned to me. "Bless him, he's a darling, but his hearing is fading."

"Yes, I need someone to find Charlie. I know they took him," Doug rambled on.

"Who took him?" As always, my curiosity got the best of me.

As Doug turned to face me, I couldn't help but notice his large eyes were almost the same color as his dark grey hair. "Doug Weaver's the name. You're that young reporter who wrote the story on the Bigfoot sighting, aren't you?"

"Yes, I am. You read it?" I asked, exhilarated to speak with someone who recognized me and my work.

"Yes, and it was a load of crap," he snapped.

And with that, I gave Maddie what I felt was a look of sorrow. Immediately she grabbed my cup for a refill.

"Eyewitness? Bug's butt!" Doug fairly shouted. "You can't pay attention to those soothsayers! They never know what they are talking about. They plant fake sightings, pictures, and such, then call the media so they can get extra exposure for their failing business. Blah-blah-blah. Most of the time, the truth is right under your nose." He paused and drifted off for a long moment, then suddenly snapped to attention, causing Maddie and me to jump. "What you need is the right case!" He whipped up a wavering index finger in the air.

I didn't care what the man said. I believed Bigfoot was real, and I would be the one to prove it.

"Mr. Weaver, I'm not a detective. I'm an investigative reporter."

"Good. I'll pay you to investigate the whereabouts of my gnome." His voice, firm and demanding as if he'd made up his mind and mine too, clearly set the stage for an offer not to be refused. "I'll pay you five hundred dollars to find him."

"Five hundred dollars?" I choked out. Who in their right mind would pay someone five hundred dollars to find a missing gnome? I eyed the aging man carefully. Aside from not hearing me correctly, I believed he might be off his rocker.

"All right, one thousand dollars and not a penny more. You come by my home tomorrow. That's 204 Brindle Lane, around ten AM. I'll be expecting you." Before I could say another word, he reached into his pocket, pulled out a wad of money, rolled off two twenty-dollar bills, and set it on the table. "I'll take care of his tab as well. Keep the change, Maddie. The schnecken was the best today."

"Thank you, Doug. Don't worry. You'll get Charlie back safe very soon." For reasons I couldn't explain, Maddie's expression touched my heart.

"Charlie?" I whispered to her as I gave Doug a nod when he walked past me and out of hearing range.

"All of his gnomes have names."

I had the crazy sensation that this case as it was a bad idea.

"Listen, Doug has one of the most elaborate flower gardens in this state. He's won countless garden contests, and several of his roses have their own subgenus, named for him or his wife. Flowers are his life's work, especially since his wife passed away a few years ago. The flowers and gnomes are all he has these days."

"Oh, wow. I didn't know. I'm sorry to hear about his wife. So, he's genuine and not—" I twirled my index finger around the side of my head.

"Doug's all there." She tapped her temple. "He misses his wife something awful. I think that's why he's a bit grumpy with new people."

"What happened to her?"

"He doesn't talk about it. He mentioned she died in a camping accident, but talking about it stresses him too much, so I let him be. I respect people, you know?"

Maybe I was a bit soft-hearted, but Doug seemed to have seen some tough times. He appeared to be the sweet grandfather type who always had a stash of candy or cookies around the house for the neighborhood kids. How could I refuse his generous offer?

Tomorrow, Bob McLarney had his first case to solve—the Case of the Missing Gnome.

TWO

My father always told me that if Mondays were terrible, it just meant Tuesdays would be better. Even though I lost my job yesterday, I took my father's advice and remained hopeful for today's offer. A few people think I live with my head in the clouds. Much like my father's way of life, I choose to believe there is goodness in the world despite what people say.

Maybe it was that cup of coffee at Maddie B's or the fact I had my first real gig, even if it was a missing garden artifact, but today I felt like I could conquer the world.

I strolled into Maddie B's with a broad smile, a pep to my step, and a song in my head. The local radio station had decided to play a particular theme for their morning eighties devotional hour. And now that song had glued itself to every brain particle I possessed.

"Hey'ya, Bob!" Maddie looked up from the cash register just as she finished ringing up a customer. Her gentle smile drew me in like a soft breeze on a sweltering summer day.

I gave her a smile followed by a gentlemanly nod as I hopped a seat at the counter. "Hey, Maddie! How's it going today?"

After a glance around the joint, I recognized the faces of all the regular morning cuppers. Unfortunately, I didn't have any names to go with their faces, but I'd only been in this village for two weeks. I'd know each one by name and occupation, given a little more time.

Maddie placed a cup that contained magical delight in front of me, wiped the counter with a white bar towel, folded her arms on the counter, and leaned closer. "Same as always. You seem particularly happy this morning."

The warm cinnamon and subtle sensual myrrh tones carried by her perfume were a welcome change to the previous day's nasal disaster. Maddie always smelled nice.

I shot her a wink and slowly sipped the coffee. "Perfect as aways." I pressed the paper napkin to my lips, then gave her an appreciative smile. "Say, what else can you tell me about Mr. Weaver?"

"Well, he's an interesting person, Douglas Weaver. He likes to be called Doug. He has quite the green thumb, and since his wife, Luna, passed, roses have become his specialty. Luna loved roses. Rest her soul."

"Is his interest in flowers a hobby or job?"

"A little of both. Doug sells his rosebuds to Amelia's Things and Teas. She uses the buds to make a special tea blend for her customers."

"Like you make the coffee special for each of your customers?" I grinned, then took a sip.

Her eyelids lowered as a soft red glow kissed her cheeks. "In a way, yes. But you don't seem like a tea kinda guy to me, Bob."

I loved the way she said my name, for what it was worth. Her voice had that warm effect on me that made me believe everything in the world would be okay. I was positively sure that she had that effect on all her customers.

"I don't?" I lifted my brows and sat straight.

"Nope. See, I can tell a thing or two about people."

"Perceptive, are you?"

She frowned slightly, then gently tucked a long strand of her dark red hair behind her ear. "Intuitive sounds better." Maddie stood as one of the cuppers walked up to the register. "Everything good, Frank?"

Ah, yes. A perfect way to put a name with the face. Frank, a medium height, blond, blue-eyed, and handsome man, looked to be in his mid- to late forties. I gathered from the fresh-pressed royal blue slacks, white collared shirt, and grey/blue striped tie he was a professional. Judging by the black Rockport Men's Essential shoes he wore. My best guess was he was a doctor. They were the same brand and make of shoes my father wore to his medical office every day. I remember him saying that you could tell a lot about a man by his shoes. My father had many sayings, most of which didn't make sense, but they stuck with me nevertheless.

Upon leaving, the good man glanced in my direction and nodded before he exited to the outside.

Maddie returned, refilled my cup, did her magic sugar and spoon routine, and tapped the spoon lightly. There was something special about her. I just couldn't put my finger on it.

"Frank," I began after I knew the man was out of hearing range. "Is he a doctor?"

"Yes, Dr. Stein works at the hospital when he's not working at his clinic. He's the best doctor in town. How could you tell?"

I gave a little shrug. "I can tell a thing or two about people," I said with a grin. "Just intuitive, I guess. But back to Doug—yesterday you mentioned that all his gnomes have names. How many does he have?"

"Three, I think. Charlie was the last one he got for the new flowerbed. He was excited about him since he was a special order and all. I'm sure he'll show you around and introduce you to them."

"Okay." I hesitated for a long moment and said a silent prayer that I wouldn't have to talk to a stone or plastic statue to appease my eccentric new client.

As if Maddie had read my mind, she laughed. "Doug's a nice man. He does take the gnomes very seriously, though."

Maddie made a good point. If Doug took the gnomes seriously, it might help if I knew more about them before talking to Doug.

"Good to know." I reached in my pocket, pulled out a five-dollar bill, and left it on the counter. "I'd better be on my way. I still have time to do some research on the gnomes before meeting with Doug."

"Now, that's a good plan. Good luck, and I'll see you tomorrow, Bob." Her pleasant smile always warmed my heart as much as the coffee.

Once outside, I strolled back to my apartment. I still had a couple of hours to spare before meeting Doug, so out came the phone, and the research began.

I quickly typed in "gnomes" and hit the search button. All sorts of information popped up, from the types of gnomes, where to buy them, prices, and finally, their history. Apparently gnomes were considered nocturnal, mythical creatures who used to protect buried treasure; but these days they were used to protect crops and gardens. Well, that information should be helpful in Doug's case. Another interesting fact I found hard to believe was that gnomes moved around until spotted by a human. In consideration of the possible existence of Bigfoot—I supposed anything was possible.

No…just no.

As hard as I tried, I couldn't believe that little statues came to life. However, I had to keep an open mind if I were to find Doug's missing gnome, Charlie.

At precisely 9:58 AM, I drove up before two large black iron gates set into a brick wall that surrounded the property. I pressed the buzzer and sat silently while waiting for a response. I noticed security cameras on either side of the iron gates. However, if Mr. Weaver had security cameras, he might have seen what happened to Charlie. I couldn't believe they would overlook the video footage.

"Yes?" A male voice spoke over the intercom.

"I have an appointment with Mr. Weaver. It's Bob McLarney."

"Certainly." The voice from the intercom spoke with a lofty accent I recognized as classic "British butler." Mr. Weaver must have more money than I imagined.

The large gates opened slowly, and I drove through, admiring the well-built, solid construction of the wall. I wasn't sure whether the wall was meant to keep something or someone out or keep them in.

Beautiful and fragrant concolor firs, trees native to Wisconsin, lined both sides of the blacktopped driveway, adding appeal and charm to the place. I recognized those trees from my childhood home; they were my mother's favorites. The lush greenery and perfectly manicured lawns flanking the short drive were remarkable.

As half-expected, Doug lived in a red brick mansion complete with a marble fountain in the center of the driveway. I parked Emma Jean, my '65 red convertible Mustang, in front of the main entrance.

After soaking in the view of the scenery outside, I made my way up the steps to the grand double doors of the entrance, where I pressed another buzzer. The right side of the two doors opened immediately, and behind it stood a man dressed in a black uniform and white shirt. The light grey shading on the sides of his perfectly groomed black hair hinted he might be in his fifties.

"Mr. Weaver is waiting for you in the garden. Please follow me."

"Thank you." I tried to be polite, but couldn't help but wonder what a British butler would be doing in this small town.

The butler guided me down a long hall that led to an indoor sunroom adorned with many white vases filled with fragrant flowers. Comfortable blue and white striped cushions complemented the white wicker furniture. This was a room for relaxing. From there, the butler ushered me through a sliding glass door onto a smooth, pebbled-stone walkway, which led in turn to a sitting area surrounded by some of the most beautiful roses I'd ever seen: many assorted reds, whites, yellows, pinks, and even purple colors. Mr. Weaver sat at a wooden table under a white trellis covered in pink roses. On the table, a teapot and two teacups, complete with saucers, awaited. Today his cardigan was navy blue, still dusted with what I took to be pollen, and moth-eaten as well.

"Bob, please join me." He motioned to the empty chair across from him. "I do enjoy conversation before business."

"Thank you." I pulled back the chair, taking care not to scrape it against the stone flooring underneath us, and then seated myself. "This is a beautiful place you have here, Mr. Weaver."

"Thank you, and please call me Doug. Would you care for some tea? It's a delightful blend made from the buds of these roses." Doug motioned his feeble hand to the roses encamped around us, and then his attention turned to the butler. "Richard, would you bring us some of those crumpets—er, cookies—what are they called?"

"Biscuits, sir."

"Yes, the raspberry ones. I do love them so."

"Yes, sir."

Doug's attention drifted back to me. "Now then, I hope you like biscuits and tea. I'm not British, as you can probably guess, but I do love their customs, and I love rose tea." He inhaled a slow breath and leaned back into the chair. "Roses are a moth's favorite food. The buds contain beneficial vitamins and minerals for humans as well."

"I did not know that fact about moths and rosebuds. Interesting." I paused a moment to take it all in. "I detect a hint of southern twang in your accent. Where are you from?"

"You would be correct, my boy. I was born and raised in a small town called Point Pleasant, located in West Virginia. Through a series of unfortunate events, I left and found myself here with my beloved late wife, Luna."

"I'm sorry to hear about your loss." I pulled out a notepad to begin taking notes. "The roses, are they Luna's or—"

"I love roses and flowers as much as Luna. Roses are truly a way of life for me." Doug shifted positions in his chair, leaning forward as Richard approached, holding aloft a plate of raspberry-topped creamed-filled cookies, which he set on the table with a flourish.

Immediately Doug plucked one of the sweets off the plate and gestured that I should do the same.

"I've never seen anything like these cookies—biscuits." I selected one as the butler served the fragrant rose tea.

"Yes, they are a delight. I get them from Grimm's Bakery in town. He is a wonderful young man and a talented baker to boot. Richard keeps the cookies in stock for me." He took a sip of tea, then dotted his mouth with the napkin. "I have somewhat of a sweet tooth." Doug chuckled as he reached for another biscuit.

Honestly, at his age, I wondered if he still had all his teeth or wore dentures of some kind. Nevertheless, it wasn't my business.

Curiosity brought me back to the hospitality at hand. I'd never heard of rose tea. I lifted the cup to my lips and inhaled the rose, spice, and subtle citrus fragrances. Since Maddie had piqued my interest, I wanted to give it a go. Slowly I took a sip and savored the flavors.

Doug's eyes brightened with expectation as I allowed the floral and hint of citrus to flow over my tastebuds. Perhaps some people would enjoy the floral notes—not me. Of course, I wasn't an herbal tea connoisseur.

"You're not a tea drinker." Doug released a laugh and waved me off. "I thought so, but I wanted you to have a sample of what I do here. Amelia comes by once a month to pick up the rosebuds and drop off my tea. She has quite a thriving business."

"I'm sorry, but coffee is my passion. This tea is not bad, but you're right; I'm not a tea drinker."

"Yes, a few people love both coffee and tea. Most prefer one over the other. I enjoy a bold, robust coffee for the morning, then relaxing with a nice hot cup of rose tea with my evening sweets." Doug took another sip of his tea, followed by a bite of his third biscuit. "Now, enough about me. Let's hear a bit about yourself."

"Well, there's not much to tell. I grew up in Milwaukee and majored in journalism at Madison's School of Journalism and Mass Communication. After I graduated I took a job at the local press here in Mysty Haven, where I was fired yesterday for my article on

Bigfoot." Somehow I felt my life wasn't as impressive as the delicious cookies.

I popped the cookie in my mouth and devoured it in one bite. Doug lifted his grey brows, followed by a long, awkward stare. I wasn't sure if his expression was a reaction to my resume or eating habits. Ah, yes; sometimes I did have a problem devouring my food without thinking. My mother always gave me gentle reminders at the table to mind my eating habits. Quickly, I grabbed my napkin and dabbed the corner of my mouth, as Doug had demonstrated was the proper thing to do on finishing a biscuit.

Doug stared me down quietly, his lip barely touching the rim of his teacup.

Finally I shrugged, then nervously shifted my weight in the chair from one side to the other. "That's all I got."

"Well—it is what it is." Then, he sipped from his cup and gently replaced it on the matching saucer. "Let's have a view of where I left Charlie, shall we?" Doug leaned forward and pushed himself up from the chair without missing a beat.

A gentle sigh of relief swept over me as he guided me through the garden to a back corner, where the roses collaborated in a palette of colors. The white trellis, the white stone birdbath, the golden river-rock-pebbled walkway, the roses blooming in profusion . . . the setting reminded me of a picture on a Hallmark greeting card.

Doug stopped beside the birdbath and pointed to the ground beneath. "This is where I left him. When I came out here to give the roses their weekly food, I noticed Charlie missing. That was Monday morning, before I went to Maddie's for coffee."

My first guess was perhaps Charlie had been stolen. "Did you contact the police?"

Doug sent me a cold glare. "Are you serious? Of course I didn't. I don't want those bumbling dogheads anywhere near my garden. They could go off any minute and trample my flowers."

Dogheads? What did he mean?

"If someone stole him, wouldn't you want to press charges?" I ventured.

Doug sniffed, sending a slight shower of dust into the air. "In this town, we have our ways of dealing with mischief and misgivings. You stay here long enough—you'll learn. I hope you won't be on the end of either one, for your sake."

"I agree. I hate to ask, but do you have a picture of him?"

"Of course." He pulled out his cellphone, tapped it a few times, then handed me the phone.

Charlie the gnome—*oh my*.

I remembered a garden gnome in a neighbor's yard back home—a small, white-bearded caricature statue with a blue shirt, red hat, and white pants. Charlie wore blue pants, a blue shirt, a red hat, and was stretched out, reclining on one elbow in a seductive Burt-Reynolds *Cosmopolitan centerfold* pose. The infamous pose that gained Burt Reynolds much popularity back in 1972. So much Ryan Reynolds copied the pose in Deadpool 2. Of course I'm a Deadpool fan and would know these things.

And the smile on that gnome's face was mysteriously sly—as if he was up to no good.

"Wh-where did you say you bought him?" I tilted my head to the side to hide my confusion.

"You can't just buy these gnomes." Doug's quick yet sharp response changed suddenly as he turned and pointed to a hole dug into the ground. "I needed him to keep these blasted squirrels from my garden."

"I noticed at the gates you had security cameras. Is the front gate the only way into the property? Did you review the video feed of the night Charlie went missing?"

"Nothing out of the ordinary. Richard looked through the video back to the last flower feeding. No one came to the front gates."

"What about back here? Anything on those videos?"

"I don't have cameras on my gardens. Gnomes don't like videos." Doug's voice flattened as his large eyes narrowed. "I'll tell you who I think it is. It's those two Dhay sisters, Lilly and Aubri. Since they moved here, those two old biddies have tried to beat me in the National Rose Garden Contest every year. Everyone knew Charlie was my sure winner for this year's English Garden Competition."

I scribbled their names down. "Why would they steal Charlie? I mean, couldn't they just buy a gnome for themselves?"

"Gnomes like Charlie are highly sought after by people who consider gardening a way of life and not just a hobby. Plus, they are a bonus to decorations." Doug's attention wavered as Richard approached. "They are snobs when it comes to the helpful hands of gnomes."

"May I?" I motioned around the area, then proceeded when Doug gave me the go-ahead.

I walked around slowly, seeking anything that might look off, other than the squirrel holes and tiny little foot tracks. I didn't see anything. Until—I noticed a furball caught on one of the rose thorns. I leaned down and plucked it off, then held it up for Doug to see.

"Squirrels?" I presumed, and Doug nodded in agreement.

But then another anomaly caught my attention. I found a small corncob pipe next to the rose with the squirrel fuzz. I picked it up and noticed a faint, pink-colored glitter dusted over the pipe. As I held it up for Doug to see, the pink contents fell off and shimmered to the ground, but not before leaving its mark behind.

At first it was a subtle hint of fresh sunshine on a spring day. Next, my nose tingled, and then—

"A—*choo*!" Not once, but three times.

"Good gads, man! Get yourself together." Doug stepped away from me.

Richard appeared from nowhere with a box of tissues. I grabbed a couple, but Richard held his stance to give me more.

"Excuse me, gentlemen. It must be allergies. I did drive over with the top down." I blew my nose into a tissue, then watched Richard step back near Doug.

After I gathered myself, I shoved the clean tissues into my jacket pocket and deposited the used one on the silver tray Richard held out.

"Is this yours?" I handed the pipe to Doug.

"It belongs to Charlie." His eyes lifted to mine. "Here, I'll show you." Doug whipped out Charlie's picture again, then pointed to the gnome's hand that held the pipe.

"Curious. If you left Charlie over there, how did the pipe get over here? Perhaps the squirrels took it and dropped it?"

Doug gave me a blank stare, as though he didn't want to answer that question. Finally, he rubbed his chin and looked at the ground. "The squirrels could have tried to steal it. They do like shiny whatchamacallits."

"Do you know how I could get in touch with the Dhay sisters?"

"I only know they live in town. I've never been to their place, but Maddie knows more about everyone here than myself. I'm not as much of a social butterfly as the rest of the town."

"Sir, it's time." Richard tucked a solicitous hand under Doug's arm.

My focus stayed on the glitter and the distance between where I'd found the pipe and Charlie's last stand.

Doug took a couple of steps toward me, clasped a hand on my shoulder, and patted lightly. "I must go now. It was nice to get to know you. I believe you're a good man, Bob. Don't ever let anyone tell you differently. Height does not make the man."

What?

Doug handed me back the tiny pipe. "Here, take this and give it to Charlie when you find him."

There I stood, jaw dropped and completely dumbfounded as I slipped the pipe into my jean pocket. Did he think I was short? I was six-four; he'd had to reach upward to pat my shoulder. And what did size have to do with anything, anyway? My thoughts of Doug's mental stability wavered more than I cared to admit.

With that, Richard escorted me back through the long trail and to the front door. I didn't have much to go on. No cameras in the back to know what happened. No abnormal activity or uninvited guests through the front.

The only clues I had to solve this mystery were a tiny pipe, a hole dug by a squirrel, and two suspects in a case upgraded to a kidnapping of a *Cosmopolitan centerfold* gnome.

I couldn't wait to meet the elderly Dhay sisters, Lilly and Aubri.

THREE

Wednesday morning started, as usual, with coffee at Maddie B's and hope for more information on the Dhay sisters. A simple internet search didn't provide anything. It was as though they didn't exist.

"How's the case going?" Maddie sat the cup in front of me with a cheerful smile.

"I might need your help."

"Sure thing. What can I do for you?"

"Have you heard of Lilly and Aubri Dhay?"

"Oh—they're tea people. All I know is they live somewhere in town and frequent Amelia's."

"That's the tea shop?"

"It's close by. Once you leave here, turn right, go three blocks down, and make another right. Her shop is on the corner of Tanner and Belk." Maddie glanced over her shoulder at the Coca-Cola clock, then back to me. "She opens at eight."

"Got it. Thank you, Maddie. I appreciate your help."

"My pleasure, Bob. Anything to help you." Her attention shifted from me to another customer approaching the register.

I finished my coffee in one gulp, then dropped the money on the counter. No need to rush—I had no other plans. I figured I could search the Help Wanted ads or revamp my status on Go Jobs, where I'd found my previous job. Nowadays, the internet made jobs easier to find. The application process was the hard part. Fill out the application, take the required test, take a personality test, upload a resume, and finally, a cover letter. I felt these companies should give me a security clearance badge for all the work I did just to apply for their positions.

The *Mysty Haven Weekender,* the local newspaper, only ran on Sundays. Tony had hired me to assist the other reporters with their stories until I got the swing of things. Last Tuesday, my second day at work, Lady Luck had dealt me a different card.

"Bob, I need you to take over this lead story and head to Las Vegas tonight. James and Elbert are both out sick with—I don't know what. I just know I don't want whatever they have, so I ordered them to stay at home."

It was a chance in a lifetime and my moment to shine. "What's the story?"

"Elvis impersonators. You'll meet up with Lennie at Caesars Palace tomorrow at seven PM. Ask for him at the hostess desk in the dining room. I'm paying all expenses here, so don't screw it up."

"You can count on me, Tony!"

In hindsight, maybe I was a bit more excited than I should have been—but it was my first chance to prove my worth, and I was all in. However, Fate dealt me a new hand once I arrived at the hostess desk that Wednesday night.

"I'm here to see a Lennie. My name is Bob McLarney, and I'm with the *Mysty Haven Weekender*."

"Yes, Mr. McLarney, please come this way." The hostess guided me through the dining room to a table occupied by a man who looked identical to Elvis in his slightly overweight, long-sideburned, white-spangled-jumpsuit days.

The hostess introduced me to Lennie, then darted off.

"Nice to meet you." Lennie spoke in a melodic Elvis drawl. He extended his hand towards me. I accepted it, gave him a firm handshake, and took my seat across from him.

"Wow." I could barely believe my eyes. "I mean, you are the spitting image of Elvis in his late thirties. Impressive. How did you get started as an Elvis impersonator?"

Lennie nervously wiped his nose, then shrugged. "Man, it came naturally, you know. I mean, it's me. I was born this way. Little Elvis, they always called me that growing up." He coughed a bit, then took a sip of his water. "Sorry, I can never get used to the air conditioning. I grew up without it in the country." He cleared his throat again. "But you look like an honest guy. I tell you what, I got a real story for you if you'll listen."

"It's about impersonating Elvis, right?"

"No, no, no. Something better than that. You know people today still believe Elvis is alive. Some even claim they've seen him here or there."

"Well, I'm sure if they see you out in public, they'll think you're the real deal. Do Elvis fans approach you on the street?"

"Man, it happens. Look, the thing is, sometimes, what people see *is* real. I'm not talking about this fake news that everyone talks about." He lowered his voice. "I mean real," he confided. "Real. Just like you and me." He motioned from me to him.

"I'm not following, sorry."

"You know, this past weekend, I was up in Fall City, Washington. I had a chance to relax and fish at the Tall Chief campground. I was out there on my boat, just relaxing and waiting for the big one, when I caught something from the corner of my eye. I turned and almost fell off the boat when I saw it."

Okay, he had my full attention. "Saw what?"

"It was, I don't know, man, like seven feet tall or something and completely covered in hair, kinda like a grizzly. Bigfoot, man…I saw Bigfoot."

The eyes tell a lot about a person by reflecting the person's emotions. In my case, I felt my eyes bug forward and my bottom jaw unhinge and drop like some silly cartoon character. Lennie's eyes, however, didn't flinch. He just nodded gravely, utterly sincere.

"You saw *what*?" I managed in almost a panted breath. Bigfoot had always been this mysterious creature that eluded everyone except a few randos who ranked right up there with the alien abductees. Their stories sounded real, but the facts and evidence remained lacking. "You got any proof of this?"

Lennie's lip curled in an Elvis smile. "I took a couple of pictures with my cellphone, but I jumped and dropped the phone into the lake when it growled at me. You can find its large footprint in the mud next to the grey wooden dock if you go there. At least that's where I saw it last. It ran off, back towards the woods when it heard another boat approaching."

I thought the story might be a little fishy. "How do I know you're telling me the truth?"

"You don't, man. But if you're looking for a great cover story, this is it. It's better than asking me about what it's like to be Elvis." He chuckled, then rubbed his runny nose again. "Go, check it out yourself. It's a chance in a lifetime story."

I remember that evening very clearly, and of course I followed up on his claim. To my surprise, precisely beside the white graying boat dock were a large set of humanoid footprints. I took a picture with my phone, then decided I needed to get more proof, like a picture of the creature itself.

I searched around the edge of the campground pretty much all day until I almost missed my flight back to Wisconsin. I didn't see any more foot tracks, nor did I see anything of the creature. All I had was a picture of the foot impressions and an eyewitness of the beast.

Elvis Impersonator Meets the Legendary Bigfoot

The title of my article had a certain flair, I thought, but it sounded like a front-page story for the inquiring minds of tabloid readers. After rewriting my article and changing the title to better suit a local newspaper, I gave it to Tony, who, despite his best efforts to multitask while on a phone call, snatched my piece up, frowned at me, and said "*No!* Don't print this."

Tony threw the article back down on his desk and returned to yelling at the person on the phone. A couple of seconds later, he glanced up at me, riffled through the papers on his desk, snatched an article from his many piles, and said, "Print this!" before he motioned for me to leave.

In my defense, Tony didn't realize he'd given me back my own article. Either way, he did say to print it, so off I went. The report was the truth, and I had the evidence to back up the eyewitness's statement. The story made it to the printers on Friday. It made the front-page news on Sunday, and Monday I got the ax.

After about ten minutes of strolling around the block, I came upon Teas & Things, Amelia's tea shop. Tiny bells jingled to announce my arrival. Inside, the fragrance of warm vanilla and floral tones kissed the air. I detected subtle notes of fresh calla lilies behind the heavy aroma of rose. My father would always buy my mother a bouquet of calla lilies for Mother's Day. Those were her absolute favorite flower, and I could never forget that wonderful scent as it filled the living room air.

"Hello." A bright and cheery voice called out from behind a wall. "I'll be with you in a moment."

I took the opportunity to browse the tiny shop. The white and dark green striped walls were a perfect backdrop to the white wooden shelves bearing colorful boxes. The store had a modern yet contemporary feel to it. I counted at least four rows of back-to-back white wooden shelves filled with everything from various teas and tinctures to bath salts and herbal soaps.

In the back of the store, a white-trimmed glass display counter showed off several suggested groupings of a scented candle, mineral bath salts, and soothing lotion. On top of the counter, next to the register, sat a woven basket with little potato sackcloth pouches tied with a red ribbon. The description on the sign said "Share the Love," with a picture of a squirrel and a price tag of $1.99 each. I picked up one of the little totes and flipped over the label to read the ingredients. Mostly the items were assorted nuts, dried fruits, and berries, which made me realize this was a sweet treat for the neighborhood squirrels.

I bet Doug would love to see this.

"Hi!" A breathless yet perky voice drew me from my lucid trance of the tiny sacks. "How can I help you?"

A petite woman, very fair-skinned, with fine black hair cut in a short, pixie style, cheerfully bounced up to the register from around the store's back corner.

"Amelia?"

"Yes—that's me." Her lithe energy made me think she could have been a ballet dancer, while her bright demeanor made me think of Tinkerbell.

"You have a very lovely shop. The pleasant aroma when you walk through the door, I'm hoping that is available in a candle?" My lips broadened into a soft smile. "It reminds me of home. Calla lily, is it?"

"Oh," She giggled then her face flushed a bright pink. "That's my perfume. I make it myself, but yes, it is Calla lily."

"One of my mother's favorites." I cleared my throat and pulled myself back to business. "I was hoping you could help me find someone." I gave her what I thought was a warm and inviting smile. I guessed not from her slightly shocked or even startled look. I withdrew my smile, frowned as confusion swallowed my soul, then looked down for a moment.

"I—" She cleared her throat. "Who are you trying to find?" She forced out a gentle but curious smile and peered up into my face.

"I'm trying to find two sisters, Lilly and Aubri Dhay. I heard they come here often. They are flower gardeners here in town?"

"Oh—the Dhay sisters are botanical gardeners. There is a difference." She nodded emphatically.

"Really? I thought flower gardening was—well, is just gardening."

Amelia frowned slightly as she shook her head. "No, not at all. Botanists study the theory of plants, and horticulturists practice the applied science of plants. In my opinion, you can't have one without the other. But—"

A soft sigh escaped. "Everyone doesn't agree."

"I take it that the Dhay sisters and Mr. Weaver don't agree."

If my mention of Doug Weaver surprised her, she didn't show it. "I don't think they have ever agreed," she replied. "On anything. Don't get me wrong—both have beautiful gardens, and they work hard."

I laughed. "You just want everyone to work together, is that it?"

Amelia's face brightened. "Yes, I would like that. I don't like conflicts."

"That's admirable." I nodded. "Is there a way that I can reach the Dhay sisters?"

"I don't give out customer information, but—" She picked up a pink notepad and a pen. "If you want to leave me your name and phone number, I'll be happy to pass the information to them."

"Thank you." I took the pen and paper and smiled at her while contemplating what note I would leave to make them want to talk to me: Ah, yes—the truth.

I jotted my name and phone number down, followed by: "News Reporter, Floral Garden Contest winners."

I handed her the note. "I heard they've participated in many gardening contests over the years."

"Oh yes! They do have one of the most beautiful botanical gardens I've seen. The Dhay sisters open their garden gates to the public when their most exotic plant blooms. The Queen of Night only blooms once a year and in the middle of the night. It's due to bloom in three days."

"So that's why everyone is getting prepared."

"Oh yes! Loads of people come from all over to see this plant bloom. They also sell a few of their yearling flowers and herbs; Grimm's Bakery brings baked goods to sell; and I serve my special blend of floral teas. They like to give back to the community and beyond."

"Give back to the community?"

"Indeed. The event draws income to our village. Lilly manages the event and garden contests. Visitors come and stay at Barksdale's Bed and Breakfast, and the restaurants and shops all benefit from the weekend event. And Aubri does her part to help by making herbal medicine for Dr. Stein's patients."

"I get it—wow, that's an incredible idea. I look forward to the upcoming event. Thank you, Amelia, for your time, and don't forget to have the sisters give me a call. I'd love to speak with them." I gave her a little wink, then a sly smile as I turned towards the front door.

"I will! And come back again. I have nice gifts for your girlfriend," she called behind me.

I paused, then turned slightly. "I don't have a girlfriend, but I like the candles."

"Oh." Her face blushed from a pink to a bright rosy red as she covered her mouth and giggled. "First-time customers get a twenty percent discount off everything in the store."

"I'll be back for one of those candles. I do enjoy a warm woodsy aroma," I called back over my shoulder, then gave her a little wave upon exiting the store.

Candle, yes, but no herbal tea for me. Although the store smelled delightful and had many great gift ideas, I couldn't imagine why she'd suggested a gift for my girlfriend. I'd only been in this village long enough to know where to find the essentials—the coffee shop, grocery store, and newspaper office.

I'd just made it to the next building when I heard the sudden shrill of a tiny voice calling my name. I spun quickly to my side and looked up the walkway.

"Mr. McLarney!" I turned on my heel to see Amelia hanging halfway out of her shop.

"Lilly came into the store right after you left. She would love to speak with you," she called.

"Perfect!" As soon as I set my foot across the threshold, my heart shuddered to an abrupt halt.

The Classy Dame.

She came at me in strides, with more curves than a scenic road. Breathtakingly beautiful, her silky blonde hair whisked over her shoulders as she moved toward me. The black stilettos she wore didn't do her long legs justice.

I took a moment to gather my composure. This wasn't an old biddy, like Doug had described. She was young and vibrant, maybe in her late twenties or early thirties. I'd knew she didn't look like a cupper at Maddie B's, and apparently I'd been right—she was definitely a sipper.

Lilly stopped at least a foot before me. Her right hand gracefully floated up as I watched her gaze drink me in like lemonade on a hot summer's day. "Lilly."

I gently clasped her hand with mine and lifted it accordingly. My mother had taught me that a man must use proper manners when addressing a lady. Mom did have a different opinion from most on the term "lady."

"Bob, Bob McLarney."

"Charmed," she purred, then turned to Amelia and gave her a sideways smile. "You were right about this one." Her hazel-golden eyes drifted slowly back to mine. "So tell me, Mr. McLarney, what do you want from me?"

I released her hand, adjusted my collar, and cleared my throat. The room felt hotter, even though the air conditioning had been working fine a few minutes ago. "I wanted to ask some questions about your flower business."

"Well, if you are planning to interview me, wouldn't it be prudent to do that at my home?" Lilly's voice shifted from courteous to a smooth and sensual tone. "I mean, I'm sure you want to see my garden—for possible photos."

A strong yet fresh fragrance of sunshine and sunflowers swept over me and tingled my senses for a moment. The familiar scent, although pleasant, didn't appeal to my acute sense of smell. I'd never had experienced an allergy attack before now, but yet again, I found myself at the mercy of my sudden allergies. I bellowed out a sneeze of cosmic proportions without warning.

To my embarrassment, both ladies stepped back from me with astonished gazes.

Amelia clutched Lilly's arm, and Lilly clutched her heart as though I was a robber who had attempted to steal the priceless-looking necklace she wore.

Immediately, I pulled a tissue from my pocket and blew, then wiped my nose.

"Excuse me. I'm terribly sorry about that." I composed myself and returned to the task at hand, hoping the two women had calmed down. "Ms. Dhay, do you know Douglas Weaver?"

Lilly glanced at Amelia, who busied herself with something on one of the shelves, then turned back to me. "Yes, he and I compete in the same garden contest each year. Is something wrong?"

"Mr. Weaver is missing a gnome from his garden. I was wondering if you knew anything about that."

"A gnome?" She belted out a laugh. "That's what you wanted to talk to me about? That man and his gnomes. I wouldn't be surprised if it didn't escape on its own. It's horrible what he does with them."

"Horrible? What do you mean?"

She released a long sigh. "You're new here. I get it. Did he hire you or something to ask me about his missing gnome?"

"I'm investigating the gnome's disappearance, yes."

Lilly's pink lips pursed together as she slowly shook her head. "If he went missing from Doug's place, you won't find him. It's not the first gnome that's gone missing around here."

My gaze narrowed. "Wait—there've been more?"

"Oh, for the love of—" Lilly huffed. "Look, you're obviously not a cop, and you're not a detective. I feel your questions are rather annoying."

"Do I need to get the cops in on this, Ms. Dhay?"

"Be my guest. I have nothing to hide." Lilly dramatically threw her hands up in the air. "You have a lot to learn about gnomes, Mr. McLarney."

"I know they're mythical creatures who protect gardens. Ms. Dhay—Mr. Weaver hired me to do a job, and believe me, I will get the job done. Do you have gnomes in your garden? Maybe you stole the gnome from Mr. Weaver's estate and put it in your garden. After all, you said that gnomes help the garden."

"Oh, you really can't see everything around you. Listen, kid, I didn't steal anyone's gnome. I don't have a problem with digging squirrels, like Doug. There are more ways to protect a garden than using gnomes. If you'd done your homework, you'd know faeries are great protectors of gardens. So please, go back to Doug and tell that dusty old moth that Lilly sends her love. Oh, and let him know I don't have his gnome." And with that, she shot past me like a bat out of hell without even saying goodbye.

Amelia's unnerving gaze unsettled me, as though she'd just witnessed a murder. Neither of us knew what to say as we stood there staring at one another for a long moment.

Awkward.

"I'm—uh, gonna grab lunch," I rambled as Amelia snapped to attention, then busied herself rearranging a few candles on a shelf.

"Good luck, and I hope you find him," she called out as I headed out the door.

Him?

I left the store with several thoughts crashing around in my head. The foremost idea and the obvious: Lilly might not have stolen Charlie. However, I believed she knew more about Charlie than she admitted. If she didn't take him, I had the feeling she knew who did.

I couldn't shake the overwhelming sense that the people in this village were different. Their mannerisms, the way they talked about one another, seemed odd compared with other people I'd met. Maybe the classy dame was right, and I was blind to this town and its people. For now I had to trust my gut, and my stomach told me I had to eat in the current situation. A hungry Bob made even an angry Dr. Banner—aka The Hulk—look like an angel.

I could head back to Maddie's for lunch, then drop by Doug's and give him an update.

Still, her words haunted me: "He's not the first gnome that's gone missing around here."

FOUR

"I'll have the Finn Double Butter Burger with cheese, an extra order of onion rings, a side Caesar salad, and a Coke." I closed the menu and handed it back to Maddie.

"Would you like to try our pie of the day? It's Granny Grimm's Apple Pie—homemade, of course, baked with tart Granny Smith apples and served with a slice of Wisconsin Aged Cheddar."

Apple pie with cheddar cheese was my absolute favorite dessert in this state. Some people swear that state law requires restaurants to serve cheese on apple pie. It's not true, but I think it should be, because it tastes so delicious.

"Yes, please. And I might need a cup of coffee with the pie."

Maddie laughed. "I'll put your order right in."

Maddie's laugh, even her smile, warmed my heart every time. There was something special about her, and I thought maybe if I stayed in this town long enough, I would figure it out. Like everyone else in here, whatever that special was—I liked it.

The sentiment ended abruptly when the diner's door swung open with more force than necessary. I watched from my booth as two men walked through, then paused a moment as they scanned the guests. The first one, dressed in a mahogany brown shirt with tan pants and badges, had to be the sheriff of this small town. The one following close behind, dressed in a black uniform, had to be his deputy.

I'm not sure why the police made people feel uneasy. Maybe it was the fact they carried a gun, or perhaps people feared punishment for breaking the law. I noticed one distinctive and important sign: the scowls on the twosome's faces were serious. Even though I knew I hadn't done anything wrong—I hadn't been in town long enough to have committed a crime—my heart skipped a few beats when they moved in my direction.

The sheriff stopped at my booth. "Bob McLarney."

"Yes, that would be me."

"I'm Sheriff Alex Barksdale, with the Mysty Haven Sheriff's Department." He motioned to his sidekick. "This is Deputy Brian Barksdale Mysty Haven." His forefinger tapped on the gun neatly holstered at his hip.

I gave them a formal nod since they didn't offer a handshake. I assumed other means of greeting were customary in these parts. "What can I do for you, Sheriff?"

"We've had a complaint about your unwarranted investigations. Mr. McLarney, I understand that you are new to Mysty Haven. I'm also aware that your previous job at the *Mysty Haven Weekender* ended abruptly due to your investigative reporting."

"Mr. Weaver asked—"

"I'm aware of Mr. Weaver's concerns and requests. Let me make this clear—" He paused as his cellphone rang out an interesting heavy metal tune. Apparently the ring tone identified the caller, because he rushed to answer it. "What is it now? I'm busy." He listened intently as his attention faded from me to outside the window.

From my end, I heard what sounded like an older woman yelling on the other end of the phone. I couldn't tell what she was saying, but I gathered it wasn't good when the sheriff lowered his head and wiped a hand over his forehead.

"Fine!" he snapped, ended the call, and turned to the deputy. "That was MeMaw. Go over there right now and help your grandmother with the remodeling for this weekend. She's fired the remodeler, and there's no way she will find someone new on short notice."

The deputy nodded, then left quickly. Suddenly cold and filled with annoyance, the Sheriff's attention fell upon me. "Now—I'm telling you to leave Ms. Dhay alone. You're not to bother her again. Theft is a crime and should be handled by those sworn to uphold the law. Do you understand?"

"I understand." I inhaled a deep breath and released it slowly. "However, I'm just curious what leads you might've found on this case."

Barksdale's hard pretentious stare and flexed jaw muscles almost intimidated me. "Maybe the thief is right under my nose. Maybe it's you, Mr. McLarney."

I chuckled, not in a nervous way—no. I wasn't a person who liked to be threatened. I met his cold stare without blinking. "Maybe you're barking up the wrong tree, Sheriff."

The sheriff's eyes narrowed slightly, and I swore I heard a low growl rumble from somewhere in his chest or throat. I couldn't tell which. But he inched forward, close enough so I could see my reflection in his black eyes. "Are you trying to make jokes, boy?"

I never moved or blinked. "No, sir, I'm not. Just stating the facts."

"You listen to me and leave this to the professionals. Not to mention, I'll be watching every move you make, and I'll be there when you slip up." He flipped his business card out, swiped it under my chin, and then dropped the card on the table. "You got any questions—call my office." He pivoted sharply and marched off towards the door.

I looked down at the card, then picked it up and shoved it in my shirt pocket. That dame had something to hide, and I knew it.

"Here ya go." Maddie brought my food on a tray and set it before me, one plate at a time. "Everything all right?"

"Seems like Lilly Dhay didn't like me asking her about the gnome."

"That's interesting."

"What's interesting is the sheriff warned me not to speak to her again."

Maddie's brows lifted and her mouth formed a perfect O. She slid into the booth across from me. "Bob, it's probably because you're a newcomer to Mysty Haven. They just need to get to know you."

She smelled lovely today, a new perfume, something floral yet gentle, like Maddie. I wanted to compliment her but felt it inappropriate, so I grabbed for my napkin-wrapped silverware and put an appreciative smile on my face.

"Maddie, I find it a little odd that Lilly would go to that extreme if she didn't know anything about Charlie."

"Doug and Lilly don't get along because of the gardening contests. Both have different views of how gardens are to be kept. Doug believes gnomes are the best protectors. Lilly and Aubri disagree."

"Yes, she mentioned something about faeries."

"Some hire gnomes, and some rely on faeries."

Confusion set in. "Wait—we're talking about ceramic decorations here, right? Everyone acts as though these are living and breathing creatures or something. I get it if the squirrels don't like the decorations, and some people think they're tacky, like putting up tin pie pans to keep crows out of the gardens. But seriously?"

"Bob." Maddie's voice turned soft and subtle. "Have you ever considered seeing it from Doug and Lilly's point of view? Just because you can't see it doesn't mean it's not real. I mean, I'd expect you of all people to be open-minded." She tapped her finger on the table. "Your newspaper article on Bigfoot, for example."

I felt a tinge—no, it was a sharp stab to my heart. "Okay, you don't have to remind me about the fake news."

She laughed. "I never said it was fake news, Bob. I just said I don't read the newspaper because of all the fake news. Listen." She leaned closer. "If you believe Bigfoot is real, it's the same belief that Doug and Lilly have with the gnomes and faeries. Who are you to say they aren't real?"

"Gnomes and faeries are real?"

Maddie's mouth curved into a Mona Lisa smile as she slid out of the booth. "It's up to you to decide whether you want to believe them or not."

"Woman, you drive a hard bargain." I laughed.

"Just trying to put a few things into perspective for you. Mysty Haven is full of surprises, Bob. You've just got to see them through. Hang in there."

"Thanks, Maddie; I will keep that in mind." I glanced down at my food, then back to her. "It all looks delicious."

"You're welcome, Bob. Enjoy your meal, and if you need anything else, just let me know."

My mouth watering, I wrapped my large hands around the monster burger, then paused to watch Maddie walk away. My efforts didn't go unnoticed as she gave me one last look over her shoulder. I was desperately hungry but had to mind my manners in public, so I took a modest bite of the hamburger and chewed slowly.

I thought back to the situation to keep my mind busy and not devour the food in two gulps. There was a missing gnome who guarded a flower garden against squirrels. The Dhay sisters didn't use gnomes and didn't have problems with digging squirrels. Lilly had mentioned faeries, and of course, this was something I would need to research, as I had for gnomes. I didn't know anything about faeries, except they had wings.

Still, I couldn't shake the fact that Lilly had called the police on me. Whatever she was hiding, I would find her out, despite the sheriff and his deputy dog. I smelled a story in this village, and I felt determined to unravel all their secrets.

After finishing my entire lunch, pie included, I decided to take the coffee to go. There was no more time to waste; I needed to unload all the information to Doug and see what else he might know about the Dhay sisters and their faeries.

I left the diner feeling surprisingly good about myself and the day, with the reliable tonic of coffee securely in hand. The sun was high, and it was a good day to drive around with the top down on the old Mustang.

Once on the highway, a small white object caught my eye. I had already gotten the old girl up to speed when the thing came into clear focus—a squirrel carrying a sandwich on the right-hand side of the road.

What the—

The grey squirrel stood on its hind legs at the road's edge, holding a whole sandwich, top and bottom, in its mouth. When it saw me, it ran out into the middle of the road. At first, I thought the little creature would run across to the other side, but no—the closer I got, the more indecisive it became.

The suicidal squirrel bolted from the center of the road back towards the front of my car. I did the obvious, hit the brakes to slow down, and when I realized the brakes were of no use, I stomped on them harder, expecting a different result. Seconds passed as I swerved at full speed to avoid hitting the squirrel.

I found myself in a peculiar situation as the car defied my directional command and headed straight into the median. For reasons unknown to me, the steering didn't work.

I gripped the steering wheel tightly as the car crossed over the median and hurtled into oncoming traffic. There was nothing I could do but hold my breath and prepare to meet my maker as a red-cabbed semi came straight for me.

Most people would have closed their eyes. Some would have seen their life flash before them. I experienced nothing but my heart pounding hard enough to burst through my chest. My head felt light, and I figured I'd die before the truck hit me. At least I wouldn't experience the pain from the accident.

The semi blasted its horn.

From the corner of my eye, I caught a glimpse of something large and furry, followed by a loud bang against the right front end of my car.

I had hit something, but it wasn't the semi. The sudden impact sent the Mustang flying across the highway, straight across the shoulder, and down an incline, where I plowed through a fence. Confusion muddled my brain as the car cleared a few corner rows of corn and crashed into a tree.

"Hang in there—" a soft female voice spoke as I felt my body floating away into utter darkness.

FIVE

Death is a reality that I would rather face later than sooner. When I opened my eyes, I wasn't sure of anything anymore. I squinted against the white stinging light, wondering whether this was the bright tunnel some people claimed to see when they died.

Was I dead?

The pounding pain in my head reminded me I was very much alive. The piercing death ray of light from the fixture above added to my misery.

"Ah— there you are." A solid male voice spoke softly as his face slowly came into view. "I'm Dr. Stein. You had a very nasty car accident."

Yes, I recognized the face from Maddie B's. The man who wore the familiar doctor's shoes.

"Me hit me," I muttered, then realized my speech wasn't as cohesive as my thoughts. I meant to say, "Car hit thing." I frowned against the throbbing pain, and my twisted tongue still stuck on my nonsensical verbiage.

"We'll worry about what happened later. Right now you need to rest. You hit your head hard, but there is no sign of a concussion. You have a very thick skull. Good thing, because it saved your life."

I grunted. Yes, my mother had reminded me daily about my thick skull when I was a child.

"Am two K?"

I focused on the blue and white nametag as he picked up a needle and syringe. I barely made out the full name before he injected the substance into the IV tubing that ran to my arm: Frank N. Stein, MD.

"Yes, you most certainly are going to be okay," he said. "There is slight swelling on that beautiful brain of yours, but there's no need for surgery."

"Tay you."

"You are most welcome." He rested a hand on my shoulder and smiled at me. "I will give you a little something to help with headache and pain. I would like to run more tests tomorrow."

"Excuse me, doctor." A soft female voice came from behind the good doctor. "I need to ask your patient a few questions if you don't mind."

"I've given him medication, so you're not going to get much from him." The doctor stepped aside, revealing a very petite female dressed in a police uniform.

"I promise it won't take long." The stern expression on her face never changed as she inched inside the room.

"You got two minutes, max," Dr. Stein snapped, then turned and left the room.

At first impression and half drugged, I thought her too tiny to be a police officer. At best, she might have been five-two. The bulky police uniform looked unnatural on her slender frame. She wore her tawny brown hair pulled back into a ponytail, making her oval face and big brown puppy-dog eyes adorably cute.

She stepped forward to my bedside. "Mr. McLarney, I need to ask you a couple of questions."

"Yes," I replied as I glanced at the IV bag and the droplets going into my arm. Dr. Stein had forgotten to mention I might experience olfactory hallucination—in this case an annoying wet dog smell. My thoughts and memory were still unclear, not to mention my tongue remained twisted. But I wanted to explain about the squirrel.

"Squirrel sandwich," I managed.

After a long, blank stare, the officer frowned and started again. "Where were you headed?"

"Bug Weaver—suicidal squirrel." That was pretty much all I could muster.

"Doug Weaver?" She tilted her head to the side.

"Charlie . . ." I muttered as my eyes sealed shut.

***

I woke up in a dimly lit hospital room with closed blinds and an empty bed to my right. Since there wasn't a clock or even my cellphone in sight, I had no idea of the time or how long I had been in there.

Slowly, steadily, visions crept back into my memory. I couldn't be sure whether the police officer was real or had been a part of the crazy dreams I'd experienced in my induced slumber.

Not one, but several dreams, muddled with hints of reality, danced around in my head like flashes of old movies. Bits and pieces of Mysty Haven's people at Maddie B's Café, drinking coffee, eating, and having casual conversation, appeared normal. But the dream-memory shifted to me driving down the road and a furry creature hitting my car. The beast was a big—no, a giant werewolf—that came billowing out from nowhere and side-rammed my vehicle off the road.

I concluded that the dream was my brain's attempt to make sense of the accident. Maybe it had something to do with all the talk of mystical creatures, like gnomes and faeries, or maybe the wet dog smell had sparked my elusive condition, but I considered that I might've gone mad. That squirrel with the sandwich had a death wish and wanted to take me with it.

Maddie's challenge—"Who are you to say what is real and not real?"—could have lingered in my subconscious. I even wanted to take a long shot and say Bigfoot saved my life. I felt as though I was grasping for straws.

A soft knock on the door drew my attention as it opened slowly to a familiar face—the tiny female police officer from the day before—at least I thought it was the day before.

"Oh, you're awake. How are you feeling today, Mr. McLarney?"

"Alive." I laughed. "At least I can form complete sentences today. And you are?"

"I'm Officer Shauna Barksdale. I spoke briefly with you yesterday."

"Ah, yes. The accident."

"Mr. McLarney, you're one lucky man to be alive."

Lucky? I seemed to get that a lot lately. I gave her a quick once over, and confusion gnawed at my soul. "You were, um, here all night?"

"I returned this morning to relieve the officer on duty last night. The sheriff thought it would be a good idea if we had someone posted outside your door, at least until you recovered."

"Am I under suspicion of something, Officer?"

"No. But I need to ask you a couple of questions, if you don't mind. Of course, if you don't feel up to it—"

"I believe I can manage a few questions." I pushed myself up in the bed and adjusted the pillow to a relaxed state. Maybe I could get some questions answered as well. It was at least worth a try.

Officer Barksdale moved closer, her hand cautiously lingering near her sidearm. Really? She couldn't have considered me a threat in my current situation. Maybe it was just protocol, or perhaps I'd given her reason to be concerned that I didn't remember.

Her formal tone was appeasing and not nearly as threatening as the sheriff's. I glanced at her tiny hands and didn't notice a wedding ring.

"Excuse me," I said. "But are you related to Sheriff Barksdale?"

"Why yes, he is my father."

"Interesting. I'm going to take a long shot and ask if Deputy Brian Barksdale is also a relation?"

"Yes, Deputy Brian is my brother." She frowned as if annoyed. "Why do you ask?"

"Curious, mostly. I met the sheriff and deputy yesterday. I overheard that your grandmother runs the Barksdale Bed and Breakfast. MeMaw, is that right?"

"You seem quite the astute person, Mr. McLarney. I believe I'm the one who is supposed to ask the questions here." Her gentle voice turned a bit cooler than I'd anticipated from my query. "Now then, do you know of anyone who would want to cause you harm?"

"Harm?" The word breathlessly escaped my lips as I gazed into her deep, chocolate brown eyes. I'd never seen eyes that rich in color before, and suddenly I found myself foundering in them like a ship lost at sea. What was she saying? Something about my car?

"Yes, the mechanic at the junkyard looked over your car and determined that the brake lines were chewed through by a rodent, possibly a squirrel. He also said the steering system's failure was the result of tampering. So I'm curious, who would want to harm you?"

"Wait—my car is at a junkyard?"

"Yes, he declared it totaled. I'm sorry."

There it was—the light that everyone talked about. My life flashed before my eyes, bringing my most fond memories of that old Mustang. Emma Jean was my first car, a high school graduation gift from my dad. The first time I turned the key, I was utterly and unconditionally in love. When I pulled her out of the driveway for the first time, I remembered the song that was playing on the radio that day.

A single tear fell from the corner of my left eye. I tried to wipe it away before she noticed, but it was too late.

"Oh," she whispered as she reached for the tissue box and handed it to me. "I'm sorry."

"Thank you." I sniffled as I took a tissue from the box and blew my nose. "I'm sorry too. I never experienced this kind of loss before." I tried to laugh despite myself.

"I understand it's hard to deal with a loss. It must have meant a lot to you."

"She." I grabbed another tissue from the box. "She did mean the world to me. She was always there when I needed her and never failed me." My voice quivered. "She was the best, and now she's gone. My Emma Jean—*oh.*"

"I was with her when the wrecker arrived. If that means anything to you." Her expression softened and reflected sincere condolence.

"It does, thank you. I'm glad someone was there. Oh—" I inhaled a deep breath and exhaled slowly. I had to pull myself together. I was a grown man! "I didn't mean to break down like this—it's not me. Now, what happened?"

Maybe there was some hope of redeeming my manly qualities. I had no doubt that this woman wasn't interested in a man blubbering over the loss of his car. Tiny as she was, she looked tougher than nails.

"I wasn't far behind you when I noticed you swerve, then head uncontrollably towards the oncoming traffic. That's when I knew you were in trouble. You were headed straight for a semi, and no way you could have avoided a head-on collision."

"But something big hit my car and knocked it out of the way. Did you see who—"

Her eyebrows lifted. "Who?"

Confusion slapped my face hard enough to leave a hot, burning sensation that left me silent. I had caught a glimpse of something large, hairy, and fast—that was real. If I mentioned that I thought it might have been Bigfoot, then Dr. Stein might extend my stay in this hospital to a nice, padded room. I carefully considered my next choice of words. I knew I had to get out of this hospital before my Irish Luck kicked in. Truth be known—the Irish had terrible luck.

"Nothing, I guess."

"Did you speak to anyone before heading to Doug Weaver's?"

"Other than the sheriff and deputy, who warned me to leave Lilly Dhay alone. She must have filed a complaint against me for asking her questions about gnomes."

"I see. What was your reason for visiting Mr. Weaver?"

"I wanted to let him know I'd spoken with Lilly, and she didn't have Charlie."

She pulled out a pen and notepad. "Charlie is?"

"Charlie is Doug's missing gnome." As terrible as I thought it sounded, Officer Barksdale didn't seem surprised, or she didn't show it. "I heard he wasn't the first gnome to go missing here?" I ventured.

"You heard right. The last one that went missing was right before last year's garden contest."

"Did you find it? Was it Doug's?"

"Unfortunately, no; and no, it wasn't Mr. Weaver's. This gnome belonged to my grandmother. She got it for the flower garden in front of the bed-and-breakfast. We think it was a guest who stole it. There were so many people around the garden, it was hard to tell who might have stolen the gnome."

"But this year the garden event hasn't started, so it couldn't have been any visitors like last year, right?"

She nodded. "True. The garden event doesn't start until next week. That's when the summer flowers are supposed to be in full bloom. MeMaw's already booked solid."

"Officer Barksdale, do you know anything about the gnomes?" I couldn't help asking; it was a long shot, but I'd be happy for even a crumb of a clue.

"Not much, other than gnomes are highly sought after amongst the real gardeners. I did hear something about a secret society of sorts that stole the gnomes and set them free. They believed that all gnomes should live free in the woods." She lowered her voice. "You know, we even found a couple of gnomes at a cave out near Olsen's farm a few months ago. I never thought anything about it, since no one had reported anything missing or stolen. Everyone knows that gnomes go off wandering from time to time, but always come back home. We thought Olsen had put them there and left it at that. Who knows why people do what they do these days?"

"A cave?" Gnomes belonged in gardens, not caves. "What kind of cave?"

"Well, it's more like an abandoned wolves' den these days. But it's a cave that goes back into the mountain. I've always been told not to go into it further than I could see, so I don't know what's there."

"I hate to ask, but considering I don't have a vehicle at my disposal, is there a way you could take me to see this cave?"

Her right brow arched; then she gave me a slight frown as she nervously shifted her weight from one foot to the other. "Why do you want to see the cave?"

"I'm curious about the gnomes being there. Do you think the Olsens would mind if I were to go see it?" I flashed her a shy smile. "Of course, I would still need a ride to get there."

"I—guess. I mean, Mr. Olsen doesn't mind us being there. I suppose he wouldn't mind if I brought you."

"Great!" Maybe I sounded a little too excited, but I was already pulling the IV from my arm before she had put her pen and pad away.

"Wait!" she squeaked. "You can't just walk out of the hospital. There are rules."

"Okay. Then just check me out, we'll run over there, and you can bring me back here."

She pursed her lips. "This isn't a library, Mr. McLarney. It's a hospital. I can't just check you out and return you. You must have bumped your head hard in that accident."

"Doc said I had a thick skull, and I was fine."

"Thick skull? I believe it."

"Look, I really need some help here. I know it's the police's case—"

"*Wait—what?* What case?"

"Weaver's missing gnome, Charlie? The sheriff and deputy said they would handle the case." As soon as those words escaped me, I swear I saw a fire blazing in her eyes.

"Re-all-ly? No one mentioned any gnome case to me."

I shook my head, somberly, of course. "I can't see why. You seem to be the brightest one of them all. Maybe they had more important things for you to do other than hunting down a missing gnome to help an old man win a garden contest."

"Gurrrgh!" she growled. "The most they have me do is filing paperwork or answering the phone. It just so happened that they had no one else to watch you, which is why I'm here." She narrowed her eyes as if brewing a thoughtful scheme. Then she stomped her little foot. "You know what? Get your clothes together. I'm taking you over to the cave. I'll show them who's the runt of the litter!"

"Great!" Relief washed over me as I scanned the room for a closet. "Um, would you mind if—" Normally I wasn't a bashful man, and neither was I uncomfortable around women. However, I wasn't a man who flashed women my naked parts—especially a cop.

"Oh! Hang on." Her voice heightened as she moved to the closet. Quickly she claimed its contents and cast them onto the bed. "I'll, er, be right outside the door. Just whistle when you're ready."

I nodded, then waited until the door shut behind her before climbing gingerly off the bed and dressing. My clothes were soiled, bloody, and torn in places, and everything ached. But I wasn't about to stay in a medicated haze until . . . what? I didn't know. But the good doctor unnerved me for several reasons, and not one made any sense to me. Maybe it was the creepy way he talked about my beautiful brain, not to mention his suggestive name—Dr. Frank N. Stein.

Call me paranoid, but my suspicions of this town had become more alarming each day. Gnomes, faeries, and now suicidal squirrels. What pray tell would I discover next?

SIX

Be quiet and hurry up," Officer Barksdale whispered as she motioned for me to follow. "We got a clean break. The nurse behind the counter left to check on a patient. Follow me."

I hunched over, then scurried close behind her like a vampire stalking its next victim. We swept down the hall to a door labeled "Stairs." She whipped the door open, and down the stairs we went. Two flights later we made it to the ground floor.

With the police car in sight, I felt surprisingly good about leaving the hospital, but I promised myself that I would call them to make sure I settled with the billing department. Even though I had car insurance, I knew my deductibles, and I didn't have enough savings to cover the bill. I just hoped they offered payment plans.

A strong wet dog smell hit me as I opened the car door. When I turned my head to the side to catch some fresh air, I noticed the painted stamp on the side of the car: K9 Unit. Well, that explained the wet dog smell. I shook my head and gladly climbed into the car, eager to make my escape.

Tires squealing, Officer Barksdale peeled out of the hospital parking lot, taking us momentarily airborne as she jumped a pothole or two, then sped off into the distance. I held on for dear life as, in no time, we reached the interstate. No lights. No sirens. Just Officer Barksdale driving like Mario Andretti.

So much for a discreet departure.

Once Officer Barksdale settled into a steady pace in the light traffic on the interstate, I took a deep breath. I was glad she had turned on the A/C, but it didn't help with the dog smell. "How did you find out about the gnomes at the cave?" I asked her. "You mentioned that you'd seen them?"

"I pass by there when I go for a run. Sometimes I just need to get out and be myself for a little while." She glanced at me, then back at the road. "Do you like to run?"

"I get what you mean. It's nice to get outside and away from the office grind. No, I don't run, but I guess I should."

"Really?" She eyed me again. "I would have pegged you for an athlete. I guess you work out then."

"Nope. Never played sports, and I don't work out."

"Seriously? Wow. I mean, you're like all buff." She shook her head. "I guess you got good genes. My family's like that too—well, except for me. My dad and brothers are all big and bulky. Me, I turned out to be the runt. But hey, I don't let my size stop me. I can handle myself when needed." She lifted her chin proudly.

"I bet you're faster than them. I noticed the way you moved down those stairs. You didn't even lose your breath!"

She laughed, which made me laugh. "Yeah, that's one advantage I have over them. MeMaw always said just because I was the runt didn't mean I didn't have unique gifts. I guess speed is it."

"Officer Barksdale—"

"Call me Shauna, since I'm going to say I'm technically off duty at the moment." She gave me another glance with a smile attached.

"Okay, Shauna then. If you don't mind me asking, where are you from?"

"I was born and raised right here in Mysty Haven. I know my southern accent isn't the norm for the state. MeMaw says our bloodline and roots run deep, which is why we have such a thick accent." She giggled. "Wait until you talk to MeMaw, you'll see for yourself. Sometimes, when she gets all riled up, we don't even understand what she's saying."

I joined her cheerful laugh. "I think it's nice that you grew up around your grandmother. She sounds like a wonderful person."

"MeMaw? Oh, she practically raised my brother and me after we lost our mother when we were babies."

"Oh, I'm sorry to hear about your mom. I didn't know."

"Thank you, that's kind of you. It was a hunting accident. Dad never got over it. Did you grow up around your grandmother?"

A sudden pain strummed at my heart. "No, I never met my grandparents. Sadly, my adopted parents were a bit elderly and had already lost both sets of their parents before I was adopted. My adopted parents passed away before I finished collage, a few years ago. I still miss them very much."

"My condolences for your loss, Bob. So you never had the chance to know your real family. Family is essential to us. We may not all agree on certain things, but our bond is unbreakable. Didn't you ever wonder about your birth parents?"

I sighed, gazing out as we passed by a cornfield. "I did at one point and discovered there were no records on my parents. They were destroyed when the orphanage I had been placed in at birth burned down."

"That's terrible. Was it arson?"

"No, it was a lightning strike. From what I'd heard, the operations had long since shut down, and no one was around when it happened. The office and files remained in the building. Someone driving by on the highway reported seeing the flames when they called 911."

"Well, you're not at a complete loss. You know they do have DNA tests these days."

I smiled at the hope in her cheery voice. "I considered the idea but figured it wasn't worth it. I mean, the people who adopted me were great and gave me the best life I could have imagined. As far as I'm concerned, they are my parents."

She nodded as her face gleamed. "Bob, I like you. You seem to always be on the positive side of things. That's not a common trait these days. There's just so much negativity in the world. MeMaw says all that negative stuff out there is bound to cause some problems sooner or later."

"Oh, I agree." I laughed. "I have to stay positive to balance out my Irish Luck."

"So you're Irish?"

"Well, my adopted parents were of Irish descent, and they mentioned once that my parents were as well. I suppose I couldn't outrun the odds."

"That's a tall order, Bob." Shauna slowed the car down, approaching a road on the right side. "This road ends halfway into the field. From there we'll have to walk to the cave."

Thankfully, the sky was beautifully bright and clear, unlike most of the near-constant cloudy days in Wisconsin. I welcomed the change from the dimly lit hospital room to the great outdoors.

As Shauna and I walked through the field, the cave came into sight. Many questions flooded my find, one of which was clear: Why would anyone want to run out in the middle of a cornfield at night? The field reminded me of something out of a Stephen King horror novel, which sent chills up my spine just thinking about it. Halfheartedly, I became eerily aware that something might be lurking in the field, watching me—watching us.

Great; I'd just freaked myself out.

"You come out here at night?" I almost didn't believe the question had slipped out, but then again, I did have a bad habit of speaking my thoughts before I could stop them.

"Yeah." She stopped, then turned to look up into my face. Even in her police officer's boots, she only came to the middle of my chest. "Bob? Are you afraid?" Her voice rang with sarcasm.

Afraid? Should I be terrified that some *Children of the Corn* stuff might be happening in this little town? Or in this field filled with cornstalks and creepy cawing crows? Oh great, say that five times!

I laughed at myself. "Not really. Should I be?"

Shauna shrugged. "There's nothing to be afraid of out here."

"What about apex predators, like wolves, coyotes, and—"

"Coyotes?" She half growled. "Coyotes are *not* apex predators, Bob. You need to learn a few things about outdoor life."

"See the world?" I joked, trying to take the edge off her sudden hostility.

"Something like that," she grumbled as she pushed forward. "Wolves are the true apex predators. A lone wolf is dangerous, but a pack of wolves is deadly. Never forget that, Bob. It may save your life one day."

"Nice to know," I said politely as we cleared the cornfield to arrive at the cave.

The entrance, not nearly tall enough for me to walk through comfortably, appeared stamped into the side of a small mountain. As I kneeled and inspected the cave's interior, I noticed two gnomes leaning against the cave wall and what looked like a dirt path.

"I can't see much, but I do see two gnomes," I told Shauna, "and what looks to be another one in the distance. It's dark and hard to see."

"Let me." She ducked under the entrance and clicked on the flashlight she had brought. "Yes, I see another one. How did they get in here?"

I dropped to my knees and crawled through the entrance. As I gazed around the darkened cave, I caught a glimpse of tiny feet.

"Shine the light over there—where did you see the third one?"

Shauna moved the flashlight, and my breath caught. He was reclining in his alluring pose, without his pipe. Maybe I'd imagined the gnome smiling in Doug's photo, because the facial expression didn't match. Still, I was sure this was my missing party.

"Charlie!" I exclaimed.

"Mr. Weaver's Charlie?"

"I'm quite sure it's him. How did he get here?" I moved closer to examine the two-foot-tall gnome. He appeared in good shape, with no scratches or breaks.

"I have no idea. But he wasn't here last week." She shined the flashlight on the other two gnomes. "All I see is the three."

"Maybe there are more in the back?" I squinted into the rear of the cave, where the darkness met the light, but my vision failed miserably. Then I examined the sandy ground, and that's when I noticed a set of wolf tracks. They appeared to head further into the cave.

"I guess we should get these gnomes out of here and try to find their homes." Shauna had already picked up one of the gnomes and turned toward the opening.

"Shauna?" I began cautiously.

She stopped, turned to face me, and pointed to the flashlight. "Yes?"

"You said you thought this was an abandoned wolves' den, right?"

"Yes, it was."

"The wolf tracks—" I pointed to the track beside my large foot. "They look fresh."

Shauna froze, her eyes widened, and then I watched as a certain amount of horror filled her eyes. From her expression, I felt as though I was the one who needed to scream.

"Don't move, Bob." Her firm and cold words chilled me to the bone. I couldn't help myself—I was Bob McLarney; I turned around.

I'm not sure why I have a problem with not listening to people, but I do. If I had listened to her, I would have probably saved myself from a sudden hard strike that landed my still aching body against the rock wall . . .where I hit my head again, then crumpled down to the sandy floor. From that point, everything became a blurry mess.

I dare speak of the reality again, which eluded me. I heard a menacing growling sound, then heard a low growl as I saw a brown fur ball fly past me and knocked me into the stone wall. I was still unsure what it was, but I was sure of that same wet dog smell.

The monster's yelping and Shauna's growling faded further into the cave's darkness as I remained incapacitated. I couldn't feel my legs, arms, or even neck. My thoughts of this conjunction were the only thing that made me still believe I was alive.

Until I noticed the two little feet in front of my face, followed by a face that met mine.

"Bob? You look a mess!"

It spoke. Wait—it talks?

That was it, I knew at that point I must have died, and all this was a facade. I figured I might as well play along.

"Charlie? Is that you?"

"Yes, it's me." Charlie gave me a once over. "You need a doctor. That creature hit you hard."

"How'd you get here?"

"I was kidnapped, of course." Charlie straightened up and placed his hands on his hips.

"By whom? I mean, who took you from Mr. Weaver?"

"Oh, Bob, it was a dreadful thing! I felt something like a dark presence—like, a dark fae."

"A dark fae?"

Charlie frowned, then stepped closer and gazed into my eyes. "Of course, I said a dark fae. It was just dusk, and I was all set for my evening smoke when I realized I'd left my tobacco with Andy. You know he loves a good smoke as much as I do. He keeps guard of the south part of Doug's iris garden is located. Don't know if he knew what'd happened to me or not." Charlie scratched his head. "Anyway, I put my pipe down on the garden table and had started over to Andy when a squirrel came out of nowhere and grabbed my pipe. It was that squirrel and me! Oh, it was so on."

"Charlie, let's stay focused. Do you know you kidnapped you?" I pressed a finger to my temple and rubbed lightly to stave away the pain for a moment.

"Yes—right. I was getting to that part. I don't know what happened to me. Just as I grabbed the squirrel, it poofed me with a dust of some kind, and then I went all dizzy and numb. I froze solid as an ice cube and then fell straight on my face. When I came to myself, I was in this cave." Charlie clapped his hands together, then clasped them behind his back. "Don't know how I got here or by whom."

"Yeah, just like when the sunlight hits us and we turn to stone. All that snopp is true." A grandpa-looking gnome joined in, followed by a third one.

"Watch your language, Gramps," Charlie warned, then motioned to the elderly looking gnome wearing a white shirt, jeans and an oddly looking pointed grass hat. "That's Gramps, he belongs to one of the neighbors down the road. He was here when I arrived, so was Frankie over there. They don't know who snatched them up either."

Frankie appeared to be the youngest, dark haired and rose-red cheeks that almost gave him an innocent appeal. Like Gramps and Charlie, he dressed modestly in jeans and a white shirt with a green hat.

"Snopp. Snopp! *Snopp!*" Gramps dismissed Charlie with a wave. "Young whippers like Charlie and Frankie here think they know it all these days. Don't listen to them, Bob."

I felt a migraine coming on, and it wasn't good. Here I was talking with three gnomes. The last thing I wanted to do was pass out and wake up tied to the ground or something worse.

Gnomes didn't eat people—right?

"Wait—I thought you couldn't talk to humans?" I tried to rationalize this added information in the best possible way.

"We don't. We can't." Charlie looked as confused as I felt.

"Then how are you talking to me?" I managed to push myself up and lean against the cold cave wall.

"Easy now," Frankie interjected as he and the other gnome stood beside me as if they could handle my total weight. "Your kind don't take too good to the noggin knockers."

"Oh yes!" Charlie chimed in. "You remember what happened with that big one—"

"Yes—yes, he was a big'un. I can't remember his name, though." Gramps scratched his fuzzy white chin.

"Blimey! He got it with a small stone to the nob, he did!" Frankie shook his head.

And for whatever reason, they all turned to me simultaneously, leaned closer, and peered into my face.

"Aye! He'll make it," Frankie pronounced.

"Yeah, his eyes ain't all crossed and whatnot." Gramps patted my arm. "I thought it would be a close call there for a minute."

"Someone, please explain how you can talk to me!" My voice seemingly thundered through the cave.

"Bob!" Charlie bellowed out a laugh. "You're a—"

Before finishing his sentence, he and the other gnomes spun on their heel as a massive, brown furry wolf approached, licking its chops.

At that moment I knew I was a dead man, with nothing to save me but three tiny gnomes who might not even be real. Bob, a giant of a man, would be slain and probably eaten by a slavering hungry wolf.

I blinked in disbelief. There was nothing I could do but prepare my mind for the inevitable. The gnomes gradually stepped away from me as the towering wolf came closer.

Those giant teeth. Those pointy fangs! That flaring snout!

Oh, that wet dog smell!

"Daa-ah!" I yelled out. Why? I don't know, but it did make the wolf stop and study me curiously.

Before I caught my second breath, the wolf suddenly transformed into a naked Shauna. A lovely naked Shauna, to be sure, but nevertheless my mind went completely numb.

Shauna shot past me in a blur, wafting that wet dog smell with her.

Was she a werewolf?

I stared at the gnomes, and they stared after Shauna, then we all stared at one another.

"Eh, werewolves. They come in handy at times," Gramps announced. "Well, I guess this is our cue to leave."

"Wait! Charlie? Why haven't you left this cave before?"

"I'm not leaving this cave until I find my pipe. I must have lost it somewhere in here."

"We've had some nasty buggers to fight while looking for it too!" Frankie rocked back and forth on his heels.

"Just like you two snoppers! If you hadn't accidentally cracked that stone, we wouldn't have had to fight for our lives," Gramps snapped.

"Aye!" Frankie nudged Charlie's arm. "Gramps here conjured up a few creatures to scare us. We did give 'em a what for, didn't we?"

Charlie flexed his muscles. "We did. Then that's when the puppy dog crept into the cave. Look at'em he's just a baby."

They all turned to see a large dog like monster limping from the darkened cave. I blinked twice then shook my head slowly to clear the cobwebs.

"It's back!" I screamed like a girl.

"He's harmless as a newborn babe." Frankie waddled up to the creature, lifted his hand as it laid down for it's head to be scratched. "We figured he'd wandered away from his home. He heard us in the cave and came snooping in."

"Home? His eyes are glowing red! Who would own such a monster?" I shrieked while still in my girly tone.

"Dr. Frank N Stein." Shauna's voice drew everyone's attention.

"Daahhh!" I yelled again, as I hadn't heard or seen her come back into the cave. "You're a—"

"Yes, Bob; I'm a werewolf." She rolled her eyes, straightening her police uniform. "Why are you acting so surprised?"

"Maybe because I've never seen a werewolf before? You know that'd do it, right?" I hoped she might have mercy on me, meaning not kill and eat me or something unusual. I had no idea what werewolves ate, but it was always humans in the horror movies.

She laughed. "Yeah, that makes sense."

"So you mean to tell me that—" I pointed towards the monster dog, which looked more like a giant hellhound, all black and muscled up like a golem with red glowing eyes. "Is Dr. Frank N. Stein's monster?"

"Yeah, he's just a baby though. The tracks at the opening of the cave are his. I feared he'd gotten out and lost. His name is Elbert. He must have gotten out this morning and no one knew. Elbert's gotten out a couple of weeks ago after chasing a squirrel over the fence."

"Just another attempt on my life." I grumbled. "By the way, we need to find out who tried to kill me with the car accident."

"I'm still working on it, Bob." Shauna sighed and walked over to the monster puppy and tickled it's belly. "Besides, Elbert wasn't attacking you. He seen me and probably thought I was here to play with him. I go over to play with him on the weeknights that Dr. Stein is working late at the clinic."

I watched in amazement that the creature as it's hind legs began a kicking motion. Aside from Elbert looking like a large monstrous dog, he did look a bit silly when he groaned and stretched out his back leg.

"The back of the cave, I never knew what was back there, and now that I've seen it, I still don't know what it is." Lana rose slowly and looked to the back of the cave.

"Why bring the gnomes here?" I carefully stood, pausing to wait for the pounding in my head to ease, then picked up the flashlight where before-wolf Shauna had dropped it. "I want to see what's back there."

As I made my way towards the back, I heard a lot of groans and protests behind me from the gnomes. Shauna was the only one who remained right by my side as I tiptoed downward through the cave.

"Don't be frightened," Shauna began.

"I'm not." I kept my eyes on the path and shone the light on the walls now and again.

"I'll protect you." Her tiny voice, so sincere, brought a smile to my face.

"Thank you." I appreciated her efforts for the most part, but I was more unnerved by the fact that she was a werewolf than the unknown mysteries of this cave. I seriously wanted to freak out, but it wasn't the time. I had to keep my composure and stay focused.

What could go wrong with me and a werewolf in a dark, damp cave?

Once I felt the ground level, I shined the light around and to the left of us, the wall was adorned with ancient carvings. In front of us stood a stone table with pieces of something broken on the floor surrounding it.

I picked up one of the pieces and hefted it in my hand; it was painted stone. I took a step around the table and saw more stone pieces.

"What are they?" I whispered.

"They are our friends, Bob," Charlie replied somberly. "From what we gathered by the pieces, that's Marly, Oak and Chester. They belong to a nice couple on the East Side. I believe their names are Edward B and Lexianna Windsor."

"Edward B?" I turned to Charlie. "Any relation to Mr. B?"

"Goodness no. Edward Bernard Windsor, but most people just call him E.B." Charlie looked over the shattered ruble.

"I'll inform them on their loss," Shauna added somberly. "They're good people."

Skimming the light across the table, I noticed the same markings, a few stone pieces, and an ancient knife with carvings. "I know these," I said as I picked up the knife. "I remember seeing the symbols in a book that belonged to my parents. They are Celtic. This is a ritual knife." I looked from Charlie to Shauna. "I think someone must have sacrificed these gnomes."

"But why?" Shauna stepped closer, pulled out a handkerchief, and held her hand out. "Give it to me. We might lift the fingerprints and find who it is."

Gently, I placed the knife in Shauna's hands. Charlie stared at the knife and took a couple of steps back. I can't say I blamed him. After all, it was the murder weapon of his friends and possibly him.

"If you find out who, then you find the kidnapper. But I want to know why."

Moving closer to the wall, I let the flashlight illuminate each symbol. "It looks like . . ." I moved closer still and ran my hand over one of the symbols. An electric charge hummed against my fingertips, and I jerked my hand back. "Something powerful is behind there."

"I'll take some pictures." Shauna whipped out her cellphone and took several pictures before putting it away and walked over to the table behind me. "Maybe we can find them on the internet."

"We think it might be a doorway or something," said Charlie.

"Shauna? You mentioned that this used to be a wolves' den. Was it your family?"

The long pause made me turn to her. She stood behind me, her eyes swelling with tears. Again, confusion muddled my mind. I didn't think about anything else; I reached out to her, and she immediately fell into my arms. "Your mother?" I murmured.

"Yes." Shauna burst into sobs. "Dad said he found her back here."

"I'm so sorry." I did the only thing I thought was best; I just held her close and let her cry.

Charlie nodded, turned, and went back to join the others. Shauna cried in my arms for at least ten minutes before pulling herself together. She sniffled twice, then took a step back.

"I'm sorry." Her tiny hands wiped her tears away. "I'm not normally like this."

I cupped her face with my hand, tilting it up. "You suffered a loss. Never apologize for how you feel."

"It's just—it's the first time I've let those feelings go. I'm sorry it had to be around someone."

I gave her a soft smile. "I'm glad I was here for you. That's why you would come back to this cave."

Shauna nodded slowly, then half chuckled. "It's where I felt close to her."

A loud growl echoed around the cave, and Shauna went into crouch mode, ready to pounce on the intruder.

"Um—that was my stomach." I winced in embarrassment.

Shauna's eyes opened wide as she turned towards me. "You need to feed that thing before it jumps out and grabs someone. I'm taking you to MeMaw's."

"Seriously, I'll be—" Another growl rumbled, and before I could say another word, Shauna had grabbed my hand and towed me back through the cave.

"My pipe!" Charlie reminded me loudly. "I am *not* leaving without finding my pipe!"

"Oh!" I had forgotten entirely, no doubt a memory loss due to head injuries, gnomes, werewolf sightings and Dr. Frank N Stein's monster. "I have your pipe."

"Then hand it over, buster." Charlie extended his palm and tapped his foot. "Let's have it."

"I—um—" I shoved my hand into my jeans pocket. Of course, I felt ashamed that these were the same clothes I'd worn yesterday; but in this case, it was fortunate. I felt the tiny pipe in the corner of my pants pocket and pulled it out with much relief.

"There! I found it in Doug's Garden, near the rose bed. He told me to hang on to it for you."

Charlie looked over the pipe carefully, as if he expected it to be damaged. Then he patted it on his hand. "Aargh! Empty." He scowled at me for a moment.

I shook my head. "I don't smoke."

"Of course you don't. I'll leave with you both. Just take me to Finn so I can buy more tobacco. He carries the finest blend." Charlie shoved the pipe in his pocket, then marched towards the cave opening. "You'll have to carry me; remember the sun?"

"Oh yes." I shoved the flashlight into my belt, then hurried forward and picked up Charlie. Shauna grabbed Gramps and Frankie, and we carried them outside the cave. Elbert, of course followed happily along with his big self.

Charlie was right. As soon as the sun hit him, his body turned into a stone statue. The three kidnap victims now looked like any other garden gnomes you'd see in someone's yard. Heavy ones at that, I thought, as we trudged back to Shauna's car.

As soon as Shauna opened the door to the back of the cruiser, Elbert squeezed his way inside and made himself semi comfortable.

"Dr. Stein doesn't live far from here, so we'll drop him off on the way back into town." Shauna shut the door carefully, then climbed into the driver's seat.

"Where do we find this Finn?" I asked Shauna as she was backing the car up.

"There's only one place to find Finn. Maddie B's."

SEVEN

There were several reasons I didn't want to go inside Maddie B's, and most of those revolved around the fact that I hadn't showered or changed my clothes since my car was totaled and I'd crawled through a damp, musty cave. Not to mention, I probably smelled like a wet dog and had blood on my head. I may have even gotten a bit of Elbert's drool on my shoulder from him nudging me constantly with his nose. But I was starving, and Shauna was right. I'd need to eat something soon, or my stomach might jump out and grab something, or worse yet—someone.

"Hurry." Another growl rumbled louder than before, and my stomach felt like it was gnawing its way through my skin. I'd never experienced anything like this before. Then again, I'd never gone this long without eating before. The hunger pangs were the real deal—and painful additions to my other aches and injuries.

"Hang in there, Bob. We'll be there in five." Shauna gave me a hopeful look, and maybe it was a look of concern—I couldn't tell. "We'll take Charlie back to Doug's after you eat, okay?"

"Yes, that sounds good. I'll have to call Doug and let him know." I rubbed my stomach in hopes of calming it down. "How do you know about Finn?"

Shauna laughed. "Finn is the cook at Maddie B's. Oh, and just for the record, don't mention his height—he gets distraught over it."

"Why?"

"Finn is a leprechaun." Shauna glanced over at me again to see how I would take the news.

I shook my head in astonishment. "Why not, right? I mean, I had just learned that gnomes and werewolves were real. Why not leprechauns too?" Although I didn't think it was funny; I consider it a shock, and I don't know why.

Even as a small child, I created play scenarios where all the paranormal beings, like vampires, werewolves, Bigfoot, and Nessie, existed and played nicely together. I still believed that Bigfoot was real, despite what the Fake News claimed.

Did I even dare consider that if these paranormal beings were real, I was one step closer to discovering Bigfoot?

Bob McLarney believes!

It seemed this little town harbored some mystical qualities, which brought to my mind the question of Finn.

"So, Finn is short?"

"No-oo. Finn is tall, and he's kind of like you. But don't say anything about it, or about tall people—or sports." Shauna exhaled quickly. "Just don't say anything to him, period. He gets upset."

"A tall leprechaun, huh? Okay, but I must ask a question. Does he have a pot of gold?"

"Bob, seriously? *Seriously*?" she snapped. "Yes, he's very wealthy and hoards his money. He's very protective of it and his business dealings with Maddie B's. He's not just a cook. Finn is responsible for supplying the coffee beans to Maddie B's."

"Wait—what?" Now Shauna had my full attention. "You mean that delicious coffee they brew—Finn is behind it?"

She nodded. "Yes, he has some special beans he roasts and brews. MeMaw thinks—" She lowered her voice to a whisper. "Those are the same magical beans that grew the beanstalk that Jack climbed up."

"Wha—a? For real?"

"Real." She laughed. "She said that the leprechauns swore they would never let the beans fall into human hands again. They pick the beans in secret, then ship them to Finn to roast for coffee. Cool, huh?"

I couldn't control the laugh that burst forth. "I knew there was something different about that coffee. It tasted too good to be regular coffee. Now, is everyone in this town—" I wasn't sure how to address my question so it didn't offend anyone, particularly Shauna.

"Mysticals? Yes."

"Mysticals are—?"

"We identify as Mysticals to separate us from the human world. Mysty Haven is the only town in this state entirely inhabited by Mysticals. We don't consider ourselves creatures, like the Outsiders, people in the human world, call us."

"Aside from gnomes and—" I paused and motioned to Shauna. I wasn't sure what to call her type of Mystical being.

"Werewolf." She gave me a bright smile.

"How did you become a werewolf. Did you get bitten? Or—"

"No, I was borne this way. I guess you could say it's inherited. Nothing like what the movies say, though. We can't bite someone and turn them into a werewolf. It's more complicated than that."

"Inherited? Your family, the sheriff, Brian and MeMaw are werewolves?"

"Mm-hum. MeMaw's the pack leader. She's a tough one and will probably out live us all."

The Barksdales are werewolves. That explains why Doug called them dogheads. Well, on the brighter side, what better way to protect a town like Mysty Haven than a pack of werewolves. I knew this place had secrets, but nothing like this.

I must say, something about Shauna made me feel like being myself. "Werewolf, okay. What other types of Mysticals are there in Mysty Haven?"

"Let's see, we have a small coven of vampires who live on the West Side of town. You've already met the faeries, Aubri and Lilly Dhay, oh and Amelia. Well, Amelia is a pixie, but she's still considered a faery. And a few more in and around."

"And everyone here looks normal, well—like a human."

"Not everyone. There are a few who the faeries glamour to look like normal humans. They have reasons to keep their identities hidden, and we all agree it's for the best."

"Shauna?" I had to ask. I wanted to know, but I feared the worst as I prepared myself for the ultimate question. "Does Bigfoot live here as well?"

Shauna laughed and shook her head as she pulled alongside the curve in front of Maddie B's.

"Bob, you're so funny! That's why I like you. Let's get you something to eat before I become your next meal." She hopped out of the car and moved quickly around to the café's front door.

I wasn't sure how to take her answer. Maybe I just asked the wrong question. Maybe there were other small towns in each state where Mysticals existed and lived. It appeared they may have settled down and had families over the years. But where did they come from? I had so many questions.

I trailed inside, behind Shauna. She had made her way to the counter when I spotted

Maddie at the register. She smiled at the customer, then hurried to where Shauna and I seated ourselves.

"Bob!" Maddie frowned with concern. "I heard about the accident. Are you all right?"

"I'm fine, Maddie." My stomach growled again, much louder and more painful than before. "I need to eat. I'll take anything you've got ready—and keep it coming. I'm starving here," I pleaded as I clutched my arm tightly against my belly.

"Dear me—" Maddie darted behind the two silver doors.

I heard plates rattle, then spoons clacking, and she appeared through the door with a bowl of soup and a freshly baked loaf of bread.

"Here, start with this, and I'll take your orders."

"I'll have what I had yesterday, the Finn Burger with everything." I grabbed the bread and broke off the end, dipped it into potato soup, and left my manners to the wind.

"I'll have the chicken caesar salad and unsweet iced tea." Shauna politely handed

Maddie the menu and gave her a broad smile.

Maddie paused for a moment as she took the menu from Shauna, then looked sideways at me. For a second, Maddie's eyes narrowed as if she had discovered something she didn't want to know. Shauna didn't appear to notice Maddie's demeanor, as she was more interested in the bread. Maddie then vanished into the kitchen, and I tore into my food.

As the world disappeared from around me, the flavorful soup and my impressions of Mysty Haven comforted me. I polished off the delicious bread, ever curious. If everyone who lived in this small town were Mysticals, then I couldn't help but wonder—

What was Maddie?

"Maddie?" Shauna's voice echoed my thoughts.

"I'm sorry. What?"

"You mentioned Maddie's name. I didn't understand the first part of what you said because you were chewing. What about Maddie?"

"Oh!" I swallowed a large chunk of bread, then realized that Shauna had been watching me. To my surprise, she didn't even flinch or seemed bothered by my lack of manners. "Maddie has good food and coffee."

"Yes, she does." She leaned closer. "But not as good as MeMaw's." Then she giggled, which surprised me.

I smiled, and a bread crumb tumbled past my bottom lip onto my shirt. Shauna dusted it off and handed me a napkin. I couldn't help myself. She was so tiny and so sweet, like a little morsel of roast beef—I could just gobble her up in one bite!

Wait—what?

I frowned, then shook my head to clear my thoughts. I'd never had thoughts like that before—*never*! It was probably due to my exaggerated hunger that I had viewed her as a tiny roast, a delicious wolf rack of ribs, a—

What was wrong with me?

"I'm sorry." Her voice partly quivered, then she pulled away from me.

"No—you did nothing wrong. I think I might have low sugar or something." My stomach growled again, but not as bad as before.

Maddie returned with our order, and just in the nick of time. I thanked her without a moment to lose, then consumed the entire burger before Shauna had even taken a bite of her salad.

As I chewed, the world slipped away from me once again. I closed my eyes, savoring the sweet, savory, smoky cheese alongside the flame-kissed burger. The salty and tangy pickles, just crunchy enough to balance the subtly sweet and tart flavor of the tomato, melted with the lettuce and onions to render the taste more satisfying and filling. The experience was indeed a heavenly bliss.

I noticed Maddie and Shauna staring at me when I opened my eyes. I wasn't sure how long, but I must have gone comatose for a few minutes from the expression on their faces.

"Bob?" Shauna began. "You okay?"

Oh, the shame of it all.

"I—talked, didn't I?" My face felt as though it had burned an entirely new shade of red.

Maddie cleared her throat. "Bob, I have never had anyone compliment our burgers the way you did. Thank you."

"I know, right?" Shauna pushed her salad aside. "Maddie, I'll have what he's having."

Maddie released a soft laugh. "Sure thing, Shauna. I'll get that right out for you."

Shauna perked up, all smiles as she turned her attention to me. "We still need to talk with Finn."

I wiped my mouth with the napkin, then took a few sips of my soda to wet my tongue. "Yes, I suppose we should get all this out of the way. I don't even have Doug's phone number. I wanted to call him and let him know we found Charlie."

"That's okay, and we can drive over there after talking with Finn. They are normally up later over there anyway. Doug is kind of a night person. He doesn't like to be out much during the day unless it's necessary."

"That's interesting." I took another drink from my glass. "I would have thought Doug to be a day person because of his beautiful flower garden."

"Oh, no." Shauna laughed. "Doug does most of his work at night. It's rare to see him out in the daytime. If you happen to see him out in the day, it's usually something important."

"I met him right here, early in the morning. That's how I got the job to find Charlie. Is he mystical as well?"

"Doug was probably bothered by Charlie's disappearance. And yes, he is mystical. Back in his hometown they called him the Mothman. I thought you knew."

"I had no idea, but that would explain the dust on his sweater." I drew my brows together as another thought crossed my mind. "I heard he still misses his wife."

"I'm sure he does. Luna was a lovely lady. She and MeMaw were the best of friends. I remember her coming over at night and taking care of MeMaw's garden. MeMaw would always have a cup of coffee ready for

Luna, and they would sit on the porch and talk for hours." Shauna sighed. "I think it was the only time MeMaw found peace. But that was just like Luna. Wherever she was, she brought some type of peace with her."

"She sounds like a person I would have loved to meet." I watched a smile broaden on Shauna's face.

"You would have loved her, like much of the town. We were all sad to see her go."

I inhaled a deep breath and prepared myself for the inevitable question. "How did she die?"

Shauna's brows lifted as she looked straight ahead when Maddie came from the kitchen with her order. "She died in an accident. Like a moth to a flame, she got too close to a fire, and that was it. I don't think Doug ever got over it."

"You make it sound like it was Doug's fault."

"Oh no—it wasn't Doug's fault, but he blames himself. They were on a camping trip when it happened." She looked up at Maddie as the plate was set down before her. "Thank you, Maddie."

"Enjoy, Shauna. Can I get you a refill?" Maddie motioned to the empty glass.

"Oh yes, please." Shauna's tiny fingers released the glass to Maddie. "Now, this looks delicious."

"It was." I flushed, still ashamed of devouring my meal like a wildman. "I haven't had a burger like that in—" I stopped mid-sentence as I watched Shauna consume the giant burger in two bites. My bottom jaw dropped. *"Wow."*

"Mmmm," Shauna hummed as she wiped her mouth with her napkin as a proper princess would. "I'm sorry about that. MeMaw taught me to watch my eating manners in public, but I was hungrier than I'd thought."

A woman who ate like me.

I couldn't help but stare in awe. Shauna was just like me! Well, shorter, of course, and a werewolf, but I'd found someone I could relate to for the first time. At that moment, Shauna was perfectly beautiful.

Her face went from a curious gaze to a bright red. My eyes widened in surprise, and I had the sudden urge to explain my thoughts.

"I—"

Shauna's eyes softened as a silly smile crossed her lips. "Really? You think I'm beautiful?"

Oh.

"I—uh . . . Yes. Shauna, you are beautiful. Don't let anyone tell you any different. Just because we have different eating habits than others doesn't mean we aren't a part of society." I sat straight and pulled myself together as I watched her lean into the counter with her elbow on the table and hand cupping her chin.

"That is the sweetest thing anyone has ever said to me."

"Well, it's true. You should be proud of what you've accomplished." The room felt unbelievably hot, and I needed some fresh air. I glanced at the clock and figured we needed to return Charlie to Doug. "I think we should talk to Finn."

"Oh—yes, you're right. We do need to get Charlie and the others home." Shauna appeared to be a little sad, but I might have gone a bit overboard too quickly.

I caught Maddie's attention and motioned for her to come over. "Maddie, do you think we could speak to Finn?" I politely asked.

Shauna jumped in. "It's about some type of symbols and a knife we found in a cave. We think it's used for a ritual or something. I got pictures of the markings with my phone."

Maddie took a quick breath, then released it slowly. "I'll check with him. Hang tight."

Maddie disappeared behind the metal doors while Shauna and I waited in silence for her return. Shauna took the opportunity to moisten a napkin in her water glass and daub the blood off my face and head.

"Much better," she pronounced. "Now you look beautiful too."

After a couple of minutes, the silver double doors opened, and a tall, brown-haired man dressed in a chef's uniform and apron walked through. At first impression, he didn't look like any leprechaun I'd seen in pictures. Then again, had anyone ever taken a picture of a real leprechaun? At any rate, this leprechaun looked as normal as anyone I'd ever met—except maybe for his brilliant green eyes.

"You wanted to speak with me?" Finn folded his arms across his chest and met me eye to eye. "Well, go on with ya. I don't have all day." I should have expected the thick Irish accent—not that I knew what to expect about anything these days.

"We found some symbols—" I began slowly.

"I heard about your findings. In a cave, was it?" His gaze narrowed. "And how about you tell me why you were at that cave?"

"Finn, we were there because of Charlie and a couple of other gnomes," Shauna babbled.

"Gnomes?" Finn scoffed, gave me his best stink face, then shook his head. "That's a load of malarky! Gnomes don't go near that cave."

"You might want to tell that to the ones we rescued," I said, then quickly continued. "We also found a large stone where we think sacrifices were made." I motioned for Shauna to show Finn the pictures on her phone.

Shauna pulled up the pictures and handed her phone over to Finn to review. Finn carefully studied the photos, and then his gaze slowly met mine again.

"I know of the wall and the symbols. They are no concern of yours. But it's better for you to stay away from that cave." Finn's voice turned cool as he straightened to his full height again.

"We only want to know what the symbols are and why anyone would take the gnomes there to sacrificed," I said. "We suspect something called a dark faery might be involved."

Finn's gaze hardened, and then he shifted his attention to the coffee that Maddie poured into two cups in front of us.

"That's impossible." Finn's eyes drifted back to mine. "I put those runes on the wall meself. There were no Unseelie involved."

"Unseelie?"

"I don't know you, Mr. McLarney, but I know your clan. There are things in this world that tie us to another world, beyond what you can see with your eyes. There are good and bad in both this world and beyond. Wars you can't even begin to imagine. The Unseelie are the dark faeries you mentioned. There are no dark faeries in Mysty Haven."

"How can you be so sure about that?" Shauna challenged with a cold stare that sent shivers prickling up my spine.

Finn slowly turned his attention to Shauna, eyes first, followed by the head. "Because, my dear lass, I've banished them and kept them from coming into this town."

"Then explain to us about this." Shauna pulled out the knife and laid it on the counter in front of Finn.

Finn's eyes widened, and he immediately reached for the dagger, but Shauna was quicker. She snatched up the blade and wrapped it neatly back in the handkerchief.

"Don't play games with me, little one." Finn's voice lowered to a deep grumble. "I'm much older and wiser than you can ever imagine. If you got that dagger from the cave, it could only mean that someone was using dark faery magic. But I promise you—it wasn't an Unseelie."

Maybe this was more information than my mind could comprehend, but I had to put aside my views and open my mind to the possibility that I was living in a world that many people weren't aware exists. Then again, several people or Mysticals living here appeared to know more about me than I knew about myself.

"How are you so sure that it wasn't an Unseelie?" I asked Finn. "What makes you believe someone was using dark faery magic?" I had an idea that Charlie was right about sensing the dark fae magic. I wanted to see if my theory was correct.

"I told you, I put the protection runes there meself. The runes are powerful enough to keep any dark fae from entering within a hundred-mile circumference."

"Then who in this town would know how to use dark faery magic, and why?" I looked from Shauna to Finn.

Finn cleared his throat, then poured himself a cup of coffee and leaned his back against the wall. "Anyone can learn to use dark faery magic." He sipped the coffee from the cup. "But not everyone can wield the magic effectively. It would take someone who knew the difference between dark and light faery magic. Perhaps a faery."

"But there are only two faeries in this town. They are both light faeries," Shauna offered as she reached for more coffee.

"Aye. But tell me that a Seelie or light fae can't turn to the dark side."

It sounded a bit *Star Wars*-ish to me, so I decided to play along and see what would happen next. "So if a Seelie turned to the dark side, they can use dark magic. But wouldn't that make them an Unseelie? And if that is true, how can they exist in Mysty Haven?"

Finn laughed. "Aye, good one." He winked, then put his cup down. "My runes won't allow a dark fae inside this village. It wouldn't stop a light fae from practicing dark fae magic, either. So yes, it could be possible that we have a light fae who has turned to the dark side, as you say."

I looked to Shauna, and her expression seemed to mimic mine. "Why would they use that type of magic?"

Finn scratched his scruffy chin for a moment as he considered his answer. "I can only think of one reason, and this is because of their being near the cave. They are trying to open the portal to Faeland." He casually rolled his eyes. "We folk changed the name from Fairyland to Faeland a wee back to throw the outsiders off. Because of the wars between the Seelie, I sealed the portal. The Queen of Night, when in full bloom, provides the true essence to either open the portal or close it for a year. She will be in full bloom tomorrow night, so if I were you, I'd find that faery fast before she opens a doorway that will create a hell on Earth."

"Finn, you mentioned that the rune's spell sealed the portal to Faeland. Charlie said they were playing around back there and cracked the wall. Could something have gotten through? Maybe a creature instead of a dark fae?"

Finn's brows drew together as his eyes locked with mine. "Aye. If someone has been meddling with the portal, it is possible that a creature slipped through." He shook his head. "Gnomes, they are the most mischievous creatures and cause more trouble when not supervised. They are magical beings as well. I wouldn't be surprised if they didn't wreak havoc on the wall during their playful romping around in the cave."

"But if a creature came through, then that means that the runes are weakened. Am I right?" I leaned forward, placing my arms on the countertop.

Finn nodded. "Aye. The runes are weakening. The spell weakens around the time for the plant to bloom."

A chill shivered through me as I realized this was much bigger than the missing Charlie. I only knew of two faeries who lived in this little town: Aubri; and the one I considered dangerously beautiful:

The Dame.

EIGHT

Shauna dropped me off in front of the Dhays' elegant cottage, behind which was their infamous botanical garden. A small bead of sweat dribbled down my forehead as I rubbed my moist palms on my torn jeans and turned back to Shauna, who remained in the police car.

"You'll be fine. I'll drop these guys off to Doug and then come back to pick you up."

I nodded. "You did get Charlie's tobacco, right?"

"Yes, I got it. That gnome owes me for this." She laughed.

I stepped away from the car and waved as she drove away. I saw plenty of other people around, busy preparing for tomorrow night's event. A catering crew set up folding tables, then covered them with white linen tablecloths. As I moved forward through the gate, I thought it was best to blend in with everyone else, so I stepped in line and picked up a large box from one of the setup crew.

"Where to?" I asked, keeping my head down.

"Just on the other side of those tables over there." The young man gestured impatiently.

"Thanks." I had my way inside and with a somewhat believable excuse.

I was helping.

I caught a glimpse of Amelia to my left, so I hoisted the box higher to cover my face. I didn't want her to alarm the sisters, just in case they tried to call the police or something before I could speak with them.

Once I made it past Amelia's little stand filled with all her teas and soap delights, I kept my back to her as I set the box down as instructed by the long table.

"Yes, it should be a wonderful event tomorrow night," said a familiar voice.

The Dame.

My heart slammed against my chest, and I momentarily lost my breath at the sound of Lilly's precise diction. Should I try to speak with her or take the chance and speak with her sister, whom I hadn't met? Lilly could have me thrown off her property because of the police warning, but I was prepared to be convincing to get the answers I needed. I decided to confront her.

I straightened up, broadened my shoulders, and held my head high as I stepped towards her with stubbornness guiding my soul.

"Excuse me—" A subtle voice caused me to freeze mid-step.

Slowly, I put my foot down and turned around to see another stunning beauty. I had no doubt this had to be Aubri Dhay. Her tall height, slim features, and smooth, pearlescent skin reminded me of Lilly.

Although their features were similar, Aubri's dark brown hair and crystal blue eyes separated them quickly.

The crystal blue eyes weren't the only thing that set the sisters apart, however, a slight aura or slight glow about Aubri gave me the impression she was someone of importance or influence. Just being in her presence, I felt an overwhelming power and a great love and peace.

Unlike her sister's formal attire, Aburi dressed in a more natural, more becoming fashion. Her white silky sleeveless top draped nicely over her chest and loose-flowing silky pants. She wore matching golden cuff bracelets with some type of charm dangling at the end on each wrist, and a complementary gold pendant. She had pinned up her curly hair, accentuating her long, elegant neck.

"The box." She pointed at the box I had just left on the ground. "It needs to be on the other side of the table, please."

"Y-yes," I blathered, then picked up the box and moved it accordingly while she watched every move I made.

Her brown eyebrows drew together for a split second, and then a smile crossed her lips. "You're new here, aren't you?"

"Yes, I am."

When she moved, she walked with her head held high, her eyes locked to mine as she glided towards me. "I'm Aubri Dhay." She held out her hand. "It's a pleasure to meet you and to have you here at our home."

I took her hand in mine and gave it a gentle squeeze. "The pleasure is all mine. However, I don't think your sister would agree with you. I'm Bob McLarney."

Aubri's brows lifted; then her eyes combed over me as they finally settled back on my face. "Mr. McLarney, my sister and I do not always agree on everything. Our garden is available to the public, due to the event that will begin tomorrow night. Let us put those differences aside for now. I would be honored if you would be my guest."

"Not what I expected, but thank you." I gave her a half-bow, followed by a warm smile.

Aubri returned my smile, then moved around to my side and latched her arm through mine. "And just what did you expect, Mr. McLarney?"

"Bob, please." I inhaled quickly as I followed her lead down a cobblestone path through the garden. "Your sister and I didn't get off on the right foot. I half expected she would call the police and have me removed from this fine establishment."

Aubri's eyes brightened with laughter. "Very amusing. If you were concerned that we would have you removed, then your coming here must be of some importance."

"It is, I assure you." I ducked down to keep from hitting my head on the rose trellis she guided me under. After I made it through safely, I looked up and froze in awe.

The infamous botanical garden, fully enclosed in some form of glass, looked as enchanting as the ladies who cared for it. From the outside looking in, I saw the centerpiece taking her throne: the Queen of Night.

"The Queen of Night." Aubri motioned with a graceful wave of her hand. "The plant is native to the southern regions of the United States. However, we've managed to keep her temperature the same as her native land year-round."

"Impressive."

"Thank you." Aubri turned to face me. "Now, please enlighten me on your business here."

"There seem to be some concerns about a dark fae or someone practicing dark fae magic in Mysty Haven."

Aubri's smile quickly faded as her eyes widened and her mouth fell slightly open. Even her pearlescent skin appeared to lighten a shade. She stared at me for a long moment before saying anything. Then she shook her head and nervously chuckled.

"That's impossible. There's absolutely no way a dark fae can exist here in Mysty Haven. I know this for a fact."

"Aubri, I've seen the cave and know about the markings on the wall. I also know that the Queen of Night's essence aids in that protection. But what you may not know is that someone has been sacrificing gnomes in front of that portal."

She stepped away from me, lifting an elegant hand to her mouth, and stared off as if lost in thought. Eventually her attention returned to me.

"I know about the dark magic and its evils. The light faes are forbidden to practice it. It brings only death and destruction, no matter what it promises."

"Why would someone want to sacrifice gnomes with such malice?"

Aubri frowned. "Stealing another Mystical's life force is very powerful and only used when one wishes to summon a powerful dark being." Her eyes met mine again, only this time I saw the fear she tried to hide. "If it was in front of a portal, someone wants to open it."

"But why?"

She released a long sigh. "It's no secret among the people here why that portal was sealed many years ago. In my world, there is much conflict between the faeries. A war broke out between the Seelie Court and the Unseelie Court. The Unseelie prince demanded my hand in marriage to end the war, as it would unite both Courts in the hope of bringing peace to our realm."

"But you didn't marry him."

"No, I couldn't. I wouldn't. It was just a lie he proposed to control the entire realm. I escaped here with my sister and a few others. We sealed the portal so he couldn't come through, nor could he find us." Her expression turned sorrowful. "How many gnomes were sacrificed?"

"It's hard to say because the cave was so dark. I saw the remains of perhaps two or three. We rescued three more, and Officer Barksdale is returning them to their homes as we speak."

"The ritual consists of using seven Mysticals, three at a time, followed by the last one on the night that the Queen of Night blooms. If you rescued three of them—"

"Then the perpetrator's plan fails?"

"Not necessarily. If the plant does not bloom, there is no essence to continue the protection spell for another year. The portal will be opened."

"But if that is the case, then why go through this ritual of killing gnomes? Why not simply guarantee that the plant won't bloom?"

"It sounds simple in theory, but it's not. The ritual you describe would allow the perpetrator to overcome the rune-spell, pass through the cave portal, and make an offering to appease the dark fae royal court or the Unseelie court. I'm afraid that—"

"It will be the end of the world as we know it?" I offered.

Aubri's eyes sparked annoyance and fear. "It means that the dark fae prince could come into this world. Trust me, that's not what anyone wants." She released a soft sigh. "Bob, a lot of lives were lost in the process of making sure I got out alive. You of all people should know the risks and the loss."

Me of all people?

I scratched my head and winced against the sudden pain that shot through my skull. Perhaps I had hit my head a little too often over the past couple of days.

"I honestly don't know what you're talking about." I rubbed my temple as I grimaced against the pain.

"No?" Aubri gently took my face in her hands and peered past my eyes straight into my soul. "You're right. You don't have a clue. Your lineage, as well as your history, has been removed from your mind. It's a shame. You honestly don't know who you are." She removed her hands slowly, allowing them to slide against my skin in a comforting way. "I'm truly sorry, Bob."

I shook my head, both in doubt and confusion. Now I faced more than just the end of the world, but the end of my life as I knew it. But I needed to learn the truth.

"Are you saying someone stole my memories?" I asked Aubri.

"Yes, that's exactly what I'm saying. I see traces of them, but I don't see the real you in there. Someone didn't want you to know what or who you are."

"What am I then?" I blurted out, avoiding the questions of who did this and why.

Aubri shook her head. "I'm sorry, Bob. I cannot be the one to tell you. This is something you'll have to discover on your own."

"Aubri, I believe you can tell me. You know the truth," I persisted.

"Bob, I'm over several thousand years old. Of course I know the truth. If it is any consolation"—She took my hand in hers—"as fate would have it, you have found your way back home. You were drawn to this place because we are a part of you, just as you are a part of us. This is your home, Bob. The answers you seek, you will find here in Mysty Haven. You have my word, as a princess of the High Seelie Court."

Princess?

As if my life couldn't get any more complicated or exciting in this little hideaway town. All my first impressions were correct about Aubri. For reasons I couldn't explain, her answer warmed my heart and set my soul at ease. I gazed at her, lost in her eyes, as part of me accepted her words as the truth. Another part of me doubted my luck.

I remembered talking to my adoptive parents many times, and they always gave me the same answers. I had no reason to believe I was anything but ordinary in their eyes and the eyes of those around me. Yet in this small, secluded town, filled with mysteries, legends, folklore, and mysticals…I felt like I fit in with the totally unusual crowd. I felt as though this place accepted me, the good, the bad, and the ugly. No one made fun of me here for being myself.

I inhaled a deep breath and lightly squeezed her hand before releasing it. "I'm sure I will. For now, we need to find this person and stop them before they open that portal."

"I agree." She took my arm again and we strolled toward the rose trellis. Her reassuring touch on my arm filled me with hope. I had answers to find, and knew that here I would find them.

The warm sentiment ended when I heard a familiar voice calling. "Bob? Is that you?"

Amelia hurried toward us, holding a basket of packaged herbal tea.

"Yes, I'm afraid it is I." I bowed graciously as I kept my eyes on her.

"I'm glad to see you. Are you planning to attend tomorrow night?" She batted her pixie eyelashes and fluffed her fine black hair. "Please say yes. I created something new, just with you in mind, and I was hoping you would be willing to try it."

"I've discovered that teas aren't really my thing, Amelia. But I certainly appreciate the sentiment."

"Yes, I remember. This is not tea! It's chocolate candy—with roses! Grimm's Bakery gave me chocolatier instructions, and I whipped up my first batch. It is absolutely delicious!"

Amelia's bright eyes and hopeful smile made it hard for me to say no. I glanced at Aubri, almost as if asking for her approval.

I'd never had chocolate with roses before, and I did like food—especially chocolate. Chocolate anything was my favorite.

"Since you put it that way, I would be delighted to try your new chocolate." I gave her my best smile, and with that, she jumped and squealed with joy.

"Amelia?" Aubri pressed in. "Since when did you take an interest in making chocolates?"

"Since I met Bob!" She held her high. "I have something in my shop for everyone, except him."

I blushed. "That's very thoughtful of you, Amelia," I said. "But I did tell you that I liked candles as well."

"Yes, I know you did. But I felt so bad after Lilly . . ." Her voice faded as her gaze dropped to the ground. "The way she acted towards you at my shop."

"I really must have a word with my sister." Aubri's voice turned cool. "Please, excuse me. Bob, I do hope to see you tomorrow night. And keep me posted on the turn of events, if any." Aubri slipped gracefully away, leaving me with Amelia.

"I hope she wasn't mad at you." I hadn't even considered that possibly my stretching of the truth to interview Lilly may have gotten little Amelia into trouble.

Amelia chortled. "No, of course not. Lilly and I go back many years. Say . . ." She paused and then softened her voice. "Did you find anything more about the gnome thing?"

"Only that there is someone who may be practicing dark fae magic. It seems someone has been sacrificing gnomes."

Amelia gasped. "Why do you think they would do that?" She leaned in closer.

"I'm not sure. I think it has something to do with the cave."

"Wait—what?" She perked up. "What cave?"

"The cave by that farm, I can't remember the name. That's where we found the missing gnomes."

"What?" Her eyes widened. "You found them?"

"Yes, they'd been kidnapped and taken there. We think they were going to be sacrificed for something tomorrow night."

"During the blooming of the Queen of Night?"

"I'm not sure yet." My attention drew to Aubri, who waved me over to join her alongside Lilly. "Excuse me—" I touched Amelia's arm, then darted off towards Aubri, whose face looked grimmer than the Grim Reaper at a zombie convention.

"What's wrong?" I asked.

"It seems we have a problem." Aubri sighed. "If we are correct about what this person is doing, then it means that they could strike tomorrow night."

"And by strike you mean—"

"Attempt to open that portal." Lilly offered abruptly. "Both Aubri and I must be present to assist the plant to bloom tomorrow night. We can't afford to lose our energies for anything else. As much as I don't like it, you and your little doggo friend will have to guard the portal while we are here."

"If anything happens, Bob, call me immediately." Aubri scribbled down her number. "I'll make sure you get help."

I heard a commotion looked over the faes' shoulders to see Shauna marching toward me as if on cue. I'd say she was an angry Shauna from the tousled hair and her tiny hands balled into fists.

"Bob! We need to go *now!"* Shauna screamed at me.

NINE

Shauna looked as though she could bite the head off a mad rattlesnake. She huffed and puffed all the way to the car. I climbed into the front seat of the cruiser with her.

I admit, I honestly didn't know that much about women. In my defense, I didn't have much experience with women to know, except maybe my mother growing up. I did know that people are very much different when it comes to stressful situations. Some like to ask questions to provide a solution to a problem.

"What's wrong?"

Shauna turned to me with eyes black as the bottomless pits of hell. I remained calm and positive, despite my urge to run from danger.

"My father and brother!" she growled as she started the cruiser and whipped onto the main road. "My brother insisted I meet with him because he somehow knew that I went to the cave."

"Okay, so that wasn't bad." I tried to sound positive, thinking she had overreacted.

"No? How about he knew that I took *you* to the cave? He also said that he would tell Dad, and I'd be fired." The speedometer on the police car crept higher than I wanted to know.

"Oh—that is bad. I'm sorry for getting you involved with me, Shauna."

"It's not you!" she yelled. "It's my family! They never want me to do anything remotely dangerous. They think I can't take care of myself." She snorted. "I told my brother if he told my dad, I would kick his butt."

"And what did you do?" As if I didn't already know the answer.

"What do you think?" She glanced in the rearview mirror, then back at the road as she tried to smooth her hair down. "I went woofie on him." She paused, breathing fury. "At least when he goes back to Dad, he'll have a good reason instead of the lame excuse I took you to the cave."

I tried hard not to laugh. I even drew in my bottom lip and turned my head to look out the window. Instead, my eyes filled with water as I turned back to glance at her, and I bellowed out a gut-wrenching laugh. To my surprise, Shauna cracked up laughing with me.

"What?" She laughed harder.

"You are so bad! I've seen your brother, and he's like twice your size." I could only imagine what it looked like when she rolled on him in a furball fight.

"But I'm twice as fierce. You have no idea how my brother picked on me when we were growing up. He was merciless." She chuckled some more. "I guess I grew up strong-willed. Speaking of which, I had a chance to speak with Doug after I dropped Charlie back home. He's familiar with the Queen of Night but doesn't know how the gnomes could be involved."

"Knowing, as in he knows about the Queen of Night's essence being used to keep the portal sealed? Or just knowing about the plant and its blooming process?"

She shot me a glance. "Yes to both. Doug knows everything about the plant."

"We've got bigger problems. The culprit who stole Charlie and the others did so to open the portal to another world. Now they don't have the gnomes, so the person will need something else."

"That means whoever stole the gnomes will be back at the cave tomorrow night to finish what they started. But without the gnomes, they can't open the portal."

"True," I said, holding up a finger. "But if the Queen of Night doesn't bloom, the portal will weaken anyway."

"Oh." Her voice weakened. "I get it. You think that the person involved will do something drastic tomorrow night."

"Precisely." I was glad to see we were on the same wavelength. "Aubri wants us to camp out at the cave while she and Lilly watch the Queen of Night at the botanical garden."

"And what are your thoughts?"

I arched an eyebrow. "We know our culprit has to be a fae. So we need to be in two places at once. You take the cave, and I'll stay at the garden. This way we can keep an eye on both places at the same time. If anything happens, you can call me."

Shauna pursed her lips together. "Sounds good, up to where I call you if something happens." She screeched to a stop alongside the curb in front of my apartment, then turned to me, her tiny brows knit together. "Bob, just how do you plan on getting to the cave that fast—if something were to happen? You don't even have a car."

"Hmm, I hadn't figured that one out yet." I frowned, then reached for the door handle.

Her tiny hand touched my arm, bringing my attention to her bright eyes. "Bob, take a shower and get some sleep. I'm sure we'll develop a plan before tomorrow night."

I nodded and gave her a grateful smile as I exited the cruiser. Shauna was right. There was no way that I could get to the cave if something were to happen. Then again, what could I do if something did happen? What were my plans if I confronted the person who stole the gnomes and planned to unleash hell on earth?

As I opened the door to my current residence, I noticed a little brown package wrapped neatly with a big blue bow and a note. I gathered it up and read the handwritten message, in fine, pixie-like script:

> *Hope this tea gives you a good night's sleep. Try it, and you might like it. Amelia.*

Of course I gave it a sniff, as I fondly remember the nice aroma from Amelia's shop. The subtle rose fragrance mixed with several other unidentifiable fragrances put a smile on my face. I did pick up the light, pleasant fragrance of her calla lily perfume. She must have dropped the gift off in person. I thought the gift was a nice gesture, but I did remember telling her that I didn't care for herbal teas all that much. But I made a mental note to thank her when I saw her again.

My thoughts drifted back to the current situation. Truthfully, I hadn't thought it out that far. Yes, Shauna was a police officer, and she could arrest the perpetrator, which was where most cases end. But in this case, the person knew dark fae magic, which meant they had to be a fae.

There were only three people I knew in Mysty Haven who were faeries: Aubri, Lilly, and Amelia. Plus Finn, the giant leprechaun, knew about dark fae rituals. Lilly had a motive, if she was the jealous type, to send her sister back to Faeland. But how would it benefit her, especially after all this time? Lilly controlled the botanical garden and could have prevented the Queen of Night from blooming any year she wanted to. So no, it wasn't likely to be Lilly. I had to rule out Aubri as well, because she reacted with horror at the thought of the portal opening.

The only two suspects I had were Amelia and Finn. Amelia didn't want fighting or war; she just wanted peace. That wasn't even remotely a motive. Although a bit arrogant, Finn had quite the bean business and did know the rituals. But what could his motive be? He, too, could have reversed his own rune-spell any time he wished. And he certainly wouldn't want to lose his treasure, which was the beans he roasted into that splendor-riffic coffee. Being a leprechaun, he would guard those with his life.

After I cleaned up in the shower, I laid down on my bed, balled up my pillow under my head, and closed my eyes. The bed felt cozy, comfortable, and I didn't even need to count sheep to get to sleep.

Sheep?

My eyelids snapped open, and I stared at the vague shadows on the ceiling. What if the culprit was a wolf in sheep's clothing? A werewolf in sheep's clothing? Perhaps there was more to the Barksdales than I imagined. Maybe that was why Sheriff Alex didn't want Shauna going near the cave.

But no . . . werewolves weren't fae, were they? Of course, the perp was probably someone I'd never suspected, which could be anyone in this town. I gave the pillow a push underneath my head and closed my eyes. This time, I drifted off into the wonders of dreamland.

TEN

My morning routine had been regular: a brisk walk to Maddie B's for the special coffee. The day had passed quickly, and with it no more clues or ideas. The whole town seemed on edge, as if everyone expected the worst.

Shauna, as always, had been gracious enough to give me a lift to the botanical gardens. Her father had suggested that she and her brother keep an eye on the cave while he kept an eye on me at the Queen of

Night event. Somehow Sheriff Barksdale had the notion that I was the one who had been behind the gnome kidnapping, and he was determined to prove it. At least we had one thing in common—we intended to find the person responsible tonight.

The gathering was precisely as I'd thought it would be, with cars parked along the crowded sidewalk and a crowd headed towards the Dhays' botanical gardens. As I made my way through the front gate, I noticed Amelia handing out tea samples to passersby. To my right, Aubri, in all her elegance, chatted with a few guests as I slipped past unnoticed. Quietly, I turned the corner to make my way toward the glass garden where the finale would take place.

"I see you made it. Mr. McLarney," a dry, coarse deep voice half-growled behind me.

I didn't need to turn around to know to whom that voice belonged.

"Yes, I suppose you could say I wouldn't miss it for anything." I paused to let Sheriff Alex Barksdale catch up. He was dressed in full uniform. "I see you are here as well, on duty too." I gave a warm smile to two random ladies as they strolled by.

"Yes, I'm just waiting for you to slip up." He fixed me with a glare. "It was clever of you to involve my daughter in your little scheme to cover your tracks."

"I assure you that I have no tracks to cover. But I suppose I have every right to solve this mystery and clear my name, since I'm a suspect because I'm new in town. Isn't that right, Sheriff?"

Barksdale uttered a low growl from the back of his throat. "I warned you, McLarney, to stay out of this and leave the sisters alone. I could arrest you right here and right now."

"On what grounds? This is a public event. Besides, you know as well as I do that Aubri Dhay invited me here." I smirked and lowered my voice to a whisper. "You know what I think? I think you just can't stand the fact you're wrong about me, and you'll try to find anything to pin on the new guy."

He grabbed me by the arm and clutched it tightly as he spoke into my ear. "Stay away from my daughter. We don't like your kind."

Before I could reply, Aubri sidled up behind him and sidestepped to link her arm inside of mine. "Bob, please come join me. You can help me set up for tonight. It's almost time."

Barksdale sent another low growl as I gave him a broad smile and let Aubri tow me off like a wayward ship.

"I thought I would drag you away from him before he decided to cause a scene. He's good at his job but still a hothead." Trilling a laugh, she smiled graciously at a few guests who held up their glasses as we passed.

I shrugged. "The sheriff doesn't bother me. I guess I must be immune to hotheads."

"Good." Aubri escorted me to a table covered with a white linen tablecloth and topped with a sign marked VIP. "I reserved a special place for you. Now stay put and behave yourself." And with a wink, she turned and left me to my own devices.

For a moment, I focused my attention on the plant and allow my mind to fill with all possibilities of who might be the culprit. Then I noticed something white scrunched up on the ground behind the plant. From where I sat it appeared to be a napkin, or some sort of cloth. Without hesitation I left my chair, moved quickly around the table and made my way inside the glass dome.

Inside the area was hotter than I'd expected, but not to my surprise a waded up white cloth laid on the ground near the roots of the plant. I bent down to pick it up and noticed the same glittery dust and the undeniable overly sweet smell from roses, lilies and a very sour, putrid scent.

Roses and calla lilies? The aroma appeared to be a strong perfume, yet more herbal as if a blend. I checked the ground again and noticed where the cloth had been the soil had turned a bright yellow. A foot away from the plant, I notice tiny breadcrumbs. Upon further examination, I noticed a hole that appeared to have been dug out by a tiny animal. The roots had been exposed, which I wasn't sure if that had damaged the plant or not.

I looked up and searched around for Lilly or Aubri, but only met eyes with the Sheriff who quickly marched his way into the dome and stopped in front of me with his hand on his holstered gun.

"And what are you doing in here?" He sniffed the air, then looked at the cloth then his cold glare froze me solid. "Looks like I finally caught you red handed trying to kill the plant."

"My hand isn't red." I gave my hand a once over and noticed it had turned red. "That's odd." Among one of my allergies, the only time I experienced this type of reaction was to a weed spray I used on the lawn back home. I looked from my hand to the sheriff. "Does this smell like weed killer mixed with roses to you?"

Sheriff Barksdale's brows drew together. "Yes, it does." His hand quickly slipped from near his gun to behind his back where he pulled out a set of handcuffs. "Let's go McLarney. I'm arresting you for…"

Before he could finish his sentence and even begin to read me my rights, Aubri slipped in behind him and snatched the handcuffs away. "Put those things away!"

She pushed him aside and took the cloth from my hand and looked down at the plant. "Where did you find this?"

"Near the roots." I pointed to the yellowing ground.

"Oh no." Aubri dropped down to examine the ground. "It's still wet, someone tried to poison the plant."

"And this is why I shouldn't arrest him?" Barksdale looked from Aubri to me.

Aubri's eyes lifted to Barksdale as she released a long sigh. "No, you shouldn't arrest him because he didn't have anything to do with this."

"Just how do you know that?"

"Because he's been in my sight ever since he arrived. So don't pull your overbearing attitude with me, Alex." Aubri's cool tone sent shivers up my spine.

"Who else might have been in here?" I turned to Aubri just in time to her eyes narrow at Barksdale before they softened as she looked toward me.

"No one, really. Aside from Lilly and myself, Amelia helps with the plant every year. I'm sure she wouldn't have done anything to it. She loves plants."

"Was she in here sometime today?" I peered from Barksdale to Aubri.

Aubri thought long and hard for a moment. "Yes, she does the soil prepping. We apply a special fertilizer hours before the plant is expected to bloom. It helps with the blooming process." She took the handkerchief from my hand. "This handkerchief is hers. I'm guessing she used it to wipe her hands after she applied the fertilizer and accidentally dropped it on the ground."

"But the weed killer?" Barksdale's eyes narrowed into tiny slits.

"That poses the greatest of problems. If it has gone to the roots the plant may not bloom. Perhaps Lilly and Amelia can come up with an antidote for the plant. I'm not sure…even with our magic it will be enough. These are dark hours, very dark hours." Aubri's eyes softened into a sadness that I never wanted to see again. "I still don't believe she would have done this."

"We'll find who did it." I tried to be as assuring as I could. The weakened smile on her face told me she feared the worse. "Aubri, I'll do everything I can to help."

Gently, she reached out and touched my arm and gave me an assuring squeeze. "I know you will, Bob. I appreciate you more than you know. Now, I must find Lilly." She turned to Barksdale. "You, stay put here, don't let anyone inside until Lilly and I return."

Lilly gave me an endearing look before she walked away. Barksdale shot me a blank stare as he walked outside the glass dome and positioned himself near the door. I scratched my head as I contemplated where I'd smelled that flowery fragrance before. Lost in my thoughts I walked outside the dome to get some fresh air.

"Bob! So glad to see you here." Amelia stepped in front of me without me even noticing her arrival. She gave a little bounce and clapped her hands together. "Did you, um—get my present last night?"

My jumbled thoughts were jolted as my eyes locked with Amelia's.

Present? The tea!

"I did! Thank you, Amelia, it was a lovely gift and very considerate of you. I appreciate the sentiment." I forced out a smile as I tried to keep hold of my thoughts.

"You didn't try it." Her voice quavered a bit as sadness clouded her eyes.

"I'm afraid I don't like herbal tea." I thought I'd told her earlier. "But again, it was a nice gesture."

Amelia looked confused and didn't speak for a moment as she stared blankly into my face. "I—" She cleared her throat. "Did you find Charlie?"

"Yes, we found Charlie and the other gnomes. Shauna took them home last night. I thought you knew already?" I distinctly recalled telling her we'd found the gnomes just the day before.

She shook her head. "Simply curious. Well, I, um, need to run back to my shop. I ran out of rose tea." She giggled. "Customers, they always love that rose tea. I just thought I would pop over and see if you received my gift." She turned and began to walk back towards the rose trellis, the stopped suddenly and spun around. "Why is the sheriff standing by the door?"

"Someone tried to poison the Queen of Night sometime this morning. You didn't happen to see anything did you? Aubri said you were there applying fertilizer or something earlier."

Amelia's eyes widened. "How do you know that someone tried to poison the plant?"

"Barksdale and I both caught the scent of weed killer near the plant. I noticed a white handkerchief left by the plant, which is why I went in there. I gave the handkerchief to Aubri, she said that it was yours."

"Oh," she gave a nervous giggle. "I must have dropped it in there this morning after wiping my hands from applying the fertilizer."

I nodded. "Yes, Aubri said that must have been what happened."

"But I did find this." Amelia dug in her pocket and pulled out a pink and white scarf. "I'm not sure who this belongs too."

I took the scarf from her hand and looked it over. It had a distinct wet dog smell, which reminded me of Shauna. I heard Barksdale approaching from behind, then quickly placed himself beside me as he reached for the scarf.

"Where did you find this?" His deep voice grumbled.

I handed the scarf to Barksdale, then looked to Amelia.

"I found it inside the dome this morning. Do you know who it belongs too?"

"Shauna." Barksdale's voice turned dry and coarse.

"Why would Shauna be inside with the plant?" I turned to look at the plant again, trying to make the connection between Shauna and the plant.

Could Shauna have poisoned the plant? If so, what was her motive? She had some weird connection with the cave over her mother's death, but that wasn't a reason to open the portal…unless what killed her mother was on the other side.

My thoughts abrupted ended as I heard Barksdale on the phone with Shauna. Apparently, he'd whipped his phone out and dialed her without me noticing.

"No. Get over here right now!" He snapped then ended the call. "I will ask her about this when she arrives. Brian will stay at the cave."

I nodded and made my way back to the table, where I pulled out my chair and sat down. In my heart, I knew Shauna couldn't have done this. If I was right, she could have a motive, but she wasn't a fae.

I found myself in a peculiar situation as Finn's words haunted me:

"Anyone can learn to use dark faery magic."

ELEVEN

Shauna arrived without her brother approximately thirty minutes after being summoned by sheriff Barksdale. With eyes wide and filled with concerned she moved slowly through the trellis as her attention focused on the grim face of her father.

"What is this?" Barksdale held up the pink and white scarf high enough for her to get a clear eye's view.

"My scarf!" Shauna instinctively reached for it, but not fast enough as Barksdale moved it away from her fingers.

"Why was this scarf found in the dome? Were you in there sometime today?" Barksdale's firm and demanding tone made me take a step back.

Shauna frowned as her shoulder's slumped forward. "Yes, I was inside the dome early this morning. Albert got out again, chasing squirrels, and I found him here. He was digging on the other side of the dome. I tried to pull him back, and that's when I noticed that a squirrel had dug underneath the dome wall and had a field day with the dirt around the plant." She inhaled a quick breath, then continued. "After I shifted back into human form, I ran inside the dome to get the squirrel. I took off my scarf to smack at it, but the little devil was quick and ran past me and Albert. He bolted into a run after the squirrel, and I shifted back into wolf form then gave chase again. I must have dropped the scarf when I shifted."

"Shauna," I began softly. "Did you notice anything unusual when you were there this morning? Like the scent of weed killer or fertilizer?"

She shook her head.

"You know I warned you about Albert." Barksdale growled. "He's not a pet! Especially for a werewolf."

"But dad—" Shauna whinned. "He's just a puppy."

"He doesn't belong here!" He snapped and Shauna's brown eyes faded into what I called a puppy-dog look.

"No!" Annoyed, Barksdale inhaled a deep breath. "You didn't smell anything unusual? Did you see anyone?"

"No, just Albert."

"Fine then."

"Well," I interrupted, then cleared my throat as Barksdale's black eyes met mine. "It seems that the culprit made it here after Shauna left to chase Albert."

Albert. Suddenly, I had a flash back to the furry creature that hit my beautiful Emma Jean. Was that Albert chasing after the squirrel with the sandwich? I found myself staring at Shauna as the story she told about not being far behind me when I had the accident. The creature had to have been Albert, and Shauna had chased after him. So Albert was the one who saved my life.

"What's going on?" Shauna looked from her father to me.

"Someone poisoned the plant with weed killer sometime after you left. The smell is very distinct." Barksdale added.

"Excuse me," I politely said then moved towards the rose trellis. My thoughts rambled as much as the scents around my nose.

Shauna and Barksdale had one thing in common, aside from being werewolves, they had a heightened sense of smell. Either one could trail the perpetrator like a bloodhound on a hot trail during a hunt. In my case, I could detect peculiar scents that even a werewolf couldn't.

Fee Fi Fo hmmm....Could I smell the scent of the perpetrator nearby?

As I made my way, ducking under the trellis and bobbing and weaving through the crowd, I froze solid as I finally made it to a clear view of something quite interesting. Amelia stood behind her table with all of her shop goodies. There sitting on its hind legs, a squirrel reaching out to Amelia as if it were asking for something.

At first, I didn't think too much about it. Amelia like squirrels, hence the goodie bags she carried in her shop. Only when Amelia handed the squirrel a full sandwich, the hair on the back of my neck prickled.

The squirrel took the sandwich in it's tiny hands, then opened it's mouth and clasped onto the breaded delight. Before it retreated, the creature turned to me and above all things that could happen, it waved.

Squirrel sandwich. *Amelia.*

A soft wind blew in my direction and with it brought the familiar scents of lavender, calla lilies and…weed killer.

Why didn't I see it sooner? She stood right next to me, and I didn't even notice it before. Perhaps my attention, or rather my nose had already been clouded by the heavy scent of her perfume. I remembered the day I stepped foot in her shop. Her pleasant, yet light perfume had a sense of appeal, not like today where it overpowered the senses as if covering up another odor.

"Amelia!" I called out and gave her a friendly wave. "May I have a word with you?"

Amelia gave me a warm smile, then gracefully brushed her hand over her hair. "Of course, Bob."

I briskly made my way to her table and came to a halt as the squirrel rushed away. Maybe the squirrel recognized me from the accident, if it did then I may kill two birds with one stone today.

"Squirrels," I laughed. "They're funny little creatures, aren't they?"

"Yes," she giggled. "They are most precarious creatures."

"I guess they will do anything for food." I motioned with my finger to the squirrel running away with the sandwich.

"Oh, they will. They are easily trained with food. Most like nuts and dried fruits. That one, he loves sandwiches. He'd do anything for a peanut butter sandwich." She paused to look from the squirrel to me. "Hold the preserves of course."

I lifted my brows in surprise as I tilted my head slightly to the side. "I see. I think Aubri and Lilly had a problem with squirrels here."

"They don't. I keep them out of their garden. It's pretty easy." Amelia stood straight and proud as if she'd made a great accomplishment.

"They listen to you, then?" I relaxed my brows and leaned in with a whisper. "Then you don't know about the one that got in earlier and dug around the plant?"

Amelia's eyes opened wide as she gasped for air. "What?"

She didn't fool me, so I continued the game. "I guess you must have missed training one. Maybe the squirrel who just left?"

"I don't know what you mean?" Amelia nervously laughed.

"What I mean is, I followed the breadcrumbs back to you." My gaze narrowed. "You had a good plan Amelia, but the breadcrumbs gave you away. See your little squirrel friend here made its way into the dome and decided to do a little digging around the plant. My best guess is this happened before you entered the dome and tried to poison the plant with weed killer."

"You can't prove I had anything to do with that!" Amelia snapped.

"Oh, can't I? Let's see, you admitted to me that the squirrel would do anything for a sandwich, so to do your bidding you sent the squirrel inside the dome, while Aubri and Lilly were away this morning. However, when you arrived at the dome you noticed the plants roots were exposed, but not damaged so you decided to end the plant's life once and for all with weed killer. But, that's not all is it? You were the one who stole Charlie and hoisted him off to the cave where he and his friends would be sacrificed. You are the only faery here that has glittery dust, and that dust was found where Charlie went missing. You bagged and tagged him."

"I'm not a faery!" She shouted. "I'm a pixy! I wish you people would get that right! Pixy dust is very valuable and powerful!

"You just couldn't bare it when Albert chased after that squirrel, could you? Maybe he wanted a snack?"

"He should be banished from here! Chasing my squirrels, the way he does! I hate him! I hate him and the gnomes! They act like they are the only ones who can take care of a garden!"

"So this is why you wanted to kill the gnomes? Sacrifice them for what? To prove they are less powerful than you? If you were sacrificing them wouldn't that mean their magic is more powerful than yours?"

"Arrggguh! They are not! If they were so powerful as you say, then why would I need seven of them to open the portal."

I laughed. "I thought it was six."

"Seven, you idiot! They are that weak!"

"Ahh, I see. You are the one who knows dark fae magic." I held the handkerchief up to her face. "You dropped this behind the plant, probably wiping your hands off after you poured out the weed killer. It has the faint scent of roses from your shop and the calla lily perfume that you wear. Deny it!" I hissed.

"If that squirrel would have done it's job properly the first time, you wouldn't be here asking me these horrid questions! I knew you were a snoop when I met you!" She shrilled.

"It was your squirrel who chewed through my break lines!" My voice rose to a thunder, which drew attention to us.

Appearing panic-stricken, Amelia tried to jerk her arm from me. Then she reached into the pocket of her silky dress and pulled out a sparkly powder, which she blew into my face. "You should have taken that tea, Bob. You would have slept through tonight, and perhaps for a long time after."

I blinked hard as my eyes watered and my nose itched as if I were fighting the biggest allergy attack ever. I never had any allergies before I moved to Misty Haven. "Why?" I whispered as I fought hard not to sneeze in front of a huge crowd.

"The Prince of Faeland will be mine!" she screamed and ran off through the crowd.

Without any control, the urge became too great, and I blasted a sneeze that roared throughout the land. Everyone within a fifty-foot radius froze in place and turned to find the direction of the noise.

"Stop Amelia!" I shouted. Feeling woozy, I collapsed to the ground.

With Barksdale in tow, Aubri rushed to my side and helped me to my feet. "What happened?"

"Amelia. It's Amelia, she's after the dark fae prince. She's the one who stole the gnomes," I rambled, dizzy, but slowly recovering my senses.

"It's a good thing you are so large," Aubri told me. "That powder of Amelia's would knock out a gnome for hours—even days."

"I must have sneezed most of it away." I shook my head hard. In the distance I heard people yelling, and I bolted into a run towards the noise. When I made it through the crowd, I found Amelia on the ground with Shauna on top of her. Shauna didn't waste any time with the handcuffs as she brought Amelia to her feet.

Breathless, I gave Shauna a surprised look? "How did you get here so fast? You were on the other side of the trellis by the dome with your dad."

Shauna twisted Amelia's arm behind her back and pulled her to a standing position. "I told you I was the fastest werewolf of all."

"But you're not…" I motioned up and down with my hand.

"Yeah, I don't have to be in woofy form to be fast, Bob." She laughed.

I gave her a smile and shook my head. That girl had more surprises than a box of Lucky Charms.

Aubri arrived alongside me. "Amelia, why? Why would you want that evil here?"

"He's not evil. He's pure bliss. I will be his queen, and my sacrifices proved it!" she shrieked.

Aubri shook her head and turned to Lilly, who joined us. "She has the sickness."

"We can't help her. She needs the help of the Matriarch of the Winter Court," Lilly replied, examining the struggling Amelia.

"What sickness?" I tilted my head to the side as I looked to Aubri for an answer.

"She's under a spell of sorts, due to her relations with the prince at some point and time," Aubri replied, her expression grieved. "It's impossible to get over the influence of a male fae, unless you are a fel, a female fae. Amelia is part of the faery family, but not like us. She needs treatment that we can't provide. The only one who knows how to cure the sickness is the Matriarch. She's very skilled in healing."

"How are we going to get her back to Faeland?" Shauna asked as Sheriff Barksdale strutted into the fray and grabbed Amelia's other arm.

Finn pushed through the onlookers just in time to hear Shauna's question. "I think I can help you there," he said. "But I'll need one of you ladies to join me."

Lilly shook her head. "We need both our powers to make that plant bloom."

"Lilly, go with them. I can do this." Aubri gave her sister a gentle push on the arm.

"No! Aubri, that plant will drain all your energy!" Lilly pleaded.

"Go, please. We don't have much time left, it's almost time. I promise you, I'll be fine." Aubri motioned with her hand, then turned and walked back through the crowd.

"How much time do we have before she blooms?" I checked my watch and noticed it said two minutes after ten.

Aubri turned to me. "The plant begins to bloom at midnight."

"Then we should be back before then. Hang tight until we return."

"You're going with us?" Shauna's voice perked up with excitement.

"Yes, but we need to hurry." I gave Lilly one last look. The sadness in her eyes gripped something deep within my soul. It was a look that told me that was the last time she'd ever see her sister. As I followed Shauna and Barksdale while they hauled Amelia away, my mind raced to figure out how to help Aubri. They needed someone who had a magical rapport with plants. There was only one person I knew to call.

I dug into my pocket and pulled out my phone.

"Hello?" answered the wavering, yet ornery voice.

"Doug, we need your help over here at the garden."

TWELVE

Doug didn't want to listen to what I had to say, but I insisted that the sisters didn't have anything to do with Charlie's kidnapping—it was all Amelia's doing. The only thing Doug gave me was a grunt and ended the call.

Once I finally made it to the passenger side of Shauna's police car, she snapped her head in my direction before climbing into the car.

"Where do you think you're going?"

I hesitated for a moment, then released a sigh. "I'm going with you of course. You might need my help."

Shauna's attention drew to her father as he opened the back of his car while holding tightly to Amelia. Finn quickly climbed into the back seat and assisted the disgruntled Amelia into an upright sitting position.

"My dad's not going to like this." She murmured, then looked off into space as if she were contemplating a scheme. "Get in. I'll deal with him later."

Without a second to lose, I climbed into the passenger seat and closed the door. I didn't want her to give her the chance to change her mind. One thing I liked about Shauna, when she made her mind up there was no turning back.

Lights and sirens on, we dashed forward and onto the road like a bat escaping its worse nightmare. I felt the blood leaving my face as my fingers clutched the doorhandle from sheer fear.

The quiet car ride left time for both Shauna and I to lose ourselves in thought.

She focused her attention on the road as she took turns like Daisy Duke. I managed to stay in my seat thanks to the seat belts, but when she took a hard first corner, I questioned everything about myself including my safety. We didn't have much time to spare so I dared not complain about the driving. Although my thoughts shifted as fast as the car's transmission when I found myself praying I'd make it there in one piece. I wasn't a werewolf after all.

"You can open your eyes now." Shauna giggled as I heard the car door open.

Part of me still felt the car moving, so I gradually opened my eyes to make sure I was, in fact, in one piece.

With a subtle sigh of relief, I grasped the door and slid myself out the car. Solid ground never felt so good. "What's the game plan again?"

"Finn is going to open the portal and Lilly is going to take her to see their healer."

I gave her a slight frown. "I didn't see Lilly get in the police car."

Shauna rolled her eyes. "Bob, Lilly wouldn't be caught dead in a police car. She's a High Fae and she travels by magic. Look," she pointed toward the cave where I noticed a bright light coming from within. "She's already there. Come on, let's go."

Barksdale and Finn had already walked inside the cave with Amelia, who was still complaining each step of the way. Shauna gave me a weary glance and rolled her eyes.

"Somewhat of a drama queen, hey?" I laughed as I followed behind the group and took notice of the bright orbs that hovered around the ceiling. "That's interesting," I noted as we shoved forward.

As we came closer to the back, I noticed more of the shining orbs. I guessed right away that this was a part of Lilly's magic. How she created them, I didn't know, but they were beautiful and provided enough energy to light the entire cave, including the wall that contained all the ancient markings.

"We don't have much time," Finn announced as he sprinted towards the wall.

"Hold her steady, this will only take a minute."

With Shauna by my side, we watched as Finn lightly ran his hand over the symbols. Within seconds, the ancient script glowed a blue hue, and then the wall shimmered like a gentle ocean wave. When the wave stopped a bright new world opened before my eyes.

I stood in awe as I looked out into a meadow filled with lush dark, blueish green grass with tiny pink and yellow flowers scattered in its midst. The clear sky above carried a more purple-blue color than the one in this world. Even the tall trees at the edge of the meadow appeared older, more ancient with their huge trunks and large limbs. I'd even go as far to say that the limbs appeared strong enough to hold not just a kid's treehouse but an entire house without strain.

Among the beautiful view, the place looked peaceful, as if a place that I wanted to run in the meadow or sit under the bright sun and picnic. I edged forward in my amazement, then stopped as a soft hand touched my arm.

"This is as far as you can go, Bob." Lilly's soft voice drew my attention to her saddened eyes. "It's not safe for you."

"Why?" I uttered, well it did come out more as a whine.

Finn cleared his throat. "Bob, I mentioned wars, remember? It's not safe for anyone in Faeland who's not considered a Fae."

Before I could respond with my next question, my attention turned towards a man who galloped towards the portal on a white horse.

"Who's that?" I turned to Lilly, who's face lit up as a broad smile crossed her lips.

"Jontyer." Her voice turned into a whisper, but by the way she smiled as her eyes softened, I believed he meant something to her.

Jontyer stopped just on the other side of the portal as the horse whinnied and took a couple of steps back. Anyone with eyes could see that Jontyer wasn't just any Fae, he was a High Fae. He wore a white and gold robe, golden cloth-like boots, a gold woven belt wrapped around his waist as well as a gold head band. Maybe it was the sword that hung from his side that intimidated me, then again, his rugged, yet handsome looks didn't waver from his long, silky white hair. Indeed, he wore the noble look well.

"Lilly." Jontyer spoke softly and bowed his head as he greeted Lilly with a gentle smile. "I came as soon as I heard the alarm for the gate. I'm glad to see it is you."

"It's good to see you, Jontyer." Lilly closed her eyes, slightly bowed her head then motioned to Amelia. "We need to take her to the Magistar. She suffers from a dark fae illness.

"She must have contracted it from the dark fae prince." Jontyer looked from Lilly to me, then frowned slightly. "I'll take her, it's too dangerous for you to enter the city at this time."

Finn took the struggling Amelia from Barksdale as Jontyer dismounted his horse. Part of me thought he might have slung his silky blond hair to the side when it fell over his shoulder, but he didn't. Jontyer walked up to the portal and waited, his towering height amazed even me. He had to be at least six foot seven or more. I'd heard that elves were tall, which made me wonder if elves and faes were the same, if not related.

"She's a wild one." Finn gripped Amelia tightly as he walked her through the portal.

"I'm sure I can manage." Jontyer took her face into his hand and stared deeply into Amelia's eyes. "She'll not resist me."

"What's he doing?" I whispered, leaning closer to Lilly.

"He's putting her under a spell, so he can take her to the Magistar." Lilly spoke softly as she placed a hand on my arm. "It's better that we leave now. Amelia will get the help she needs."

I watched as Amelia's legs weakened and she fell into Jontyer's arms like a limp leaf falling from a tree. When he swooped her into his arms, that's when I noticed she appeared to be asleep.

Jontyer turned to us, then paused a his lifted his right hand. "Lilly?"

Lilly gave me a wayward smile, then slowly stepped through the portal and turned to face us. "I'll be back as soon as I can."

Jontyer waved his right hand over the portal and it closed, leaving behind the stone wall with the ancient markings.

"We need to go." Shauna's voice drew my attention away from the wall.

"What about Finn?" I frowned, then scratched my head. "How will he get back?"

"Don't worry about Finn. He knows the way back. He and Lilly will stay with Amelia until she's safe at the Magistar's." Shauna gave me a slight tug, which forced me to move forward to the path leading back to the cave's entrance.

I'd seen more magic this evening than I'd heard about in my lifetime, which wasn't that long. If someone would have told me that magic was real, I wouldn't have believed them. However, after seeing it for myself, I still questioned the reality of it all.

As I made it back through the cave, my thoughts shifted to Doug and Aubri. I only hoped he would come through for her. A small part of me knew that the cantankerous old man wouldn't resist the chance to prove to the fae that he still had what it takes to make a flower bloom.

Despite Doug's grumpy old man demeanor, I knew he had a heart of gold.

THIRTEEN

After a trail blazing ride back to the fae garden, I managed to climb out the cruiser with my dignity intact. I might have lost my heart somewhere a few miles back, but at least my head remained attached to my neck.

Shauna, Brian and I followed behind Barksdale as he bulldozed his way through the crowd. Most of the crowd had already gathered around the dome for the grand event. As I gazed around the on-lookers, the one person I'd hope to see wasn't there.

Everyone who could fit comfortably found a spot where they could watch the flower bloom. Even my ex-boss Tony and his reporters were there to take pictures. A new person, a medium height, fair skinned ginger dressed in a tan business suit and white shirt stood next to a shorter balding man with a fancy camera. While she scribbled on an electronic notepad, he took pictures of the plant and surroundings.

As I caught a clear view of the Queen of Night, it didn't look up to the part tonight. The once vibrant dark green leaves had wilted from the poison. My heart sank as I watched Aubri stand beside the plant. She gave everyone a hopeful smile and opened her arms.

"Welcome, my friends, to yet another year of the beautiful and mystical blooming cactus epiphyllum oxypetalum." Aburi gave the gazers a warm smile and continue. "Or as we lovingly refer to as the majestic Queen of Night."

"As most of you know, the plant only blooms at night and only once a year. We've taken great strides to keep her at her health so she may once again shine her beauty for all to see." Aubri then lifted her chin upward, gazed at the full moon above for a long moment, then returned her focus on the gathered crowd. "It is time."

Everyone responded by holding their wine or champagne glass high in the air. I, on the other hand, could only wonder what I could do to help. I felt desperately lost as I watched a soft shimmering glow encircle Aubri, then flow into the ground surrounding the plant.

The plant reminded me of milkweed, a curly thick vine with wispy tendrils covering the many immaculate white buds. A second or two later, the guests gasped as the buds slowly opened, revealing the white flower inside. The splendor of the moment didn't last long, as the blooming process came to a sudden halt.

Aubri closed her eyes for a moment then inhaled a deep breath. She folded her arms across her chest and trembled as if drawing upon the last bit of energy she could grasp.

"Oh, get on with it!" a grumpy old voice said as the crowd parted.

The dusty old grey man looked me straight in the eye. "You made a good point. Charlie agreed that we should put our feud aside and help one another."

Striding after Doug Weaver, at the height of his knees, came Charlie, Frankie, and Gramps.

"You guys made it!"

"It was the least we could do, Bob." Charlie adjusted his suspenders and kicked at the dirt a couple of times.

"Aw, take me to the plant. I ain't sitt'n here gettin' mushy for nut'n," Gramps rumbled.

Frankie's mouth flew open. "Blimey! She's a big one, she is."

"That's the Queen of Night, and yes, she is," I replied as I watched Frankie smooth out his hair.

"Nooo—I'm talking about the faery. Oooh, now that be my queen."

I shook my head and chuckled as Doug tapped Frankie on the back of the head to push him forward. They all trooped around the plant and joined Aubri.

Aubri's face brightened with a soft smile as she held out her hand to Doug. "Thank you."

Doug eyed Aubri a wink, alongside a cordial smile that caused a noticeable crinkling around his grey eyes. "Now, let's give this girl what she needs."

Doug slipped off his sweater and tossed it aside on the ground beside him. I watched in wonder as he stretched out his arms to the side and shook them over the plant. A cloud of dust fell from his hands and scattered about the plant.

I watched quietly alongside the crowd, possibly expecting something spectacular to occur from Doug's mighty dusting.

Nothing. Well, not what I had hoped to see, anyways.

The plant trembled as if touched by a cool breeze, scattering the grey dust to the grown. A soft blue glow began from the ground, the flowed upward through the plant into the leaves and nested on the silky white buds.

Aubri opened her arms again, this time a blue hue appeared on her hands, followed by a golden light that pulsated outward like a heartbeat. The light grew brighter with each beat, until it reached the leaves where it soaked right into the plant.

The Queen of Night perked up from her ill-fated doom as her leaves strengthened into a vibrant dark green. From deep inside the plant, a whirlwind of colors swirled upward through the stalk and then into the tip of the leaves. As the rainbow-colored light reached the buds, tiny yellow sparkles danced on each bud, cooing them out of their slumber.

It didn't take long before the buds started to bloom again. Gradually, one by one they opened, revealing layer after layer of satiny white petals until the Queen of Night unfolded into a breathtaking masterpiece.

Once the last bloom opened, Aubri opened a glass jar and held it over the plant as a violet-blue like ball of light emerged from the plant's center.

Cheers and applauses came from the crowd around me. My heart remained in my throat as I watched Aubri seal the jar which contained the essence needed to keep the portal closed. In my heart of hearts, I knew that Finn would make it back and complete the ritual.

Aubri gave Doug a warm smile. The dusty old Mothman smiled as well, the broadest smile I'd seen on his face since I'd met him. Part of me knew what it felt like to be needed by others. Doug found his place amongst the best gardeners. Gnomes, Mothman, and faeries working together for one cause. Who would have thought it possible?

Many people took pictures for varied reasons, I was sure. For me, I was simply happy to see the Queen bloom, and happy to see Aubri and Doug set aside their differences, even if only for one night.

As people chatted amongst themselves, I felt my story had ended. I'd solved the case of the missing gnome and even helped bring two enemies together. A smile crossed my lips as I nodded to myself and started to walk away. It had been a long, yet exciting night, one I would never forget.

"Where do you think you're going?" Doug's voice caught up with me. "I still owe you something."

My smile was the broadest ever as well. "You being here is more than enough payment."

"Nonsense! Don't take me for a fool! I might be old, but I'm good for my word." He dug into his coat pocket and pulled out a manila envelope. "Here, you earned every penny of it."

"Doug, really, it's too—"

"It's where you say, 'Thank you,'" he prompted with a lifting of his furred grey brows.

I laughed. "Thank you."

"I, uh—heard about your car and felt bad about that. So I made a few phone calls and, well, you have your car back and fully restored."

"How? I mean, the mechanic said the car was totaled!"

"Oh, you really don't know where you live do you, Bob? A little magic goes a long way." Doug winked, patted my shoulder, and then walked off. "She's parked out front, waiting for you!"

I stood there stunned, but happy—no, joyful—that my old girl was back with me again. I couldn't wait to see her! I opened the envelope to find one thousand dollars in fifties, and the key to my car. I pulled out the key, tossed it in the air, and beamed as I walked out to the front.

The old girl had her quirks and hadn't been the most perfect in paint or condition. But the fresh look—and I do mean she looked as though she'd come right off the showroom floor new—suited her well. My baby— Emma Jean. I opened the door and slid inside, half expecting to get that new car smell, but didn't. That was fine with me because when I turned over that motor she purred like a kitten and felt spunkier than ever.

Maybe it was time I considered Mysty Haven home. I was sure that I could find somewhere to work, maybe even as a dishwasher at Maddie B's. Then again, I didn't think I would really enjoy working with Finn; he seemed like he was too "thug" for me.

I could start a vlog on my life in Mysty Haven, gain viewers, even sponsors. I'd heard people make good money like that. But who would believe any truths I tried to talk about Mysty Haven? Plus the residents probably wouldn't want the publicity. There was still the local paper. Maybe, given the events of the night, I could speak with Tony and try to get my old job back.

As it stood, my life had endless possibilities, and the route to my success had yet to be driven. For now, it was just me Emma Jean, and the open road.

FOURTEEN

"Hiya, Bob!" Maddie's voice greeted me as I claimed my spot at the counter.

"Good morning, Maddie."

"Well, last night was sure interesting. You did a good thing, getting Doug and the sisters together." Maddie poured my coffee and worked her spoon magic, then gently pushed the cup toward me.

"Aw, I really didn't do anything. Doug just reconsidered because of Charlie."

"Stop being so modest. As much as I think he's a dear old man, Doug is stubborn. He listened to you, Bob. We've all tried to talk to him about working with the faeries, but he would get all bullheaded. Someone like yourself had to see things differently—and help him to see them differently too. That's what Doug needed." She gave me a warm smile. "He really likes you."

I felt the corner of my mouth curl up and I lifted the cup to my lips. "He's a good guy. By the way, Maddie, you know everyone in this town."

"Yes."

"Why does everyone refer to me as if I'm something different?"

"What do you mean?" She frowned and leaned against the back of the wall.

"Well, like Sheriff Barksdale mentioned I should stay away from Shauna because they don't like my kind. I don't understand what he meant."

"*Shauna?*" Maddie's right eyebrow arched. "You and Shauna?"

"*No!* Not like that—look, it's a long story." I shook my head.

"I get it. Bob, you really don't know what you are, do you?"

"Apparently, no, I don't."

"Bob, you're a giant. Well, a dwarf giant, which makes you appear normal human height. Kinda like Finn being the opposite of you—a giant leprechaun."

"I'm a giant? What the—" My mind swirled and tumbled. "There must be some mistake."

"Nope, there's no mistake. Everyone here knows it. We just assumed you did. Humans don't wander in here. They can't. Only Mysticals can find this place. Which is why we thought you already knew." Maddie tilted her head to the side. "Didn't you ever wonder why the pixie dust didn't work on you?"

"Oh, that stuff that Amelia blew in my face?"

"Yes; normally that would have turned anyone else stone cold. Pixie and even faery dust doesn't work on giants. Not everyone knows that fact, though," she added in a whisper.

"But—how? I mean, I was adopted. My parents didn't say anything to me about my birth parents being giants."

Maddie gave a little shrug. "Well, that's something new for you to uncover, now, isn't it? It's not hard to find the truth, especially here in this town. Oh! By the way, have you found a job yet?"

"No, I've been so busy with the case of the missing gnome that I haven't had the chance to even look. Why do you ask?" I wasn't sure I could manage even thinking about a job, now that I knew I was a part of the Mystical crew at Mysty Haven.

Me, a giant. That explained a lot about my eating habits and why my mother constantly reminded me to mind my manners in public.

"Excuse me," came a soft, yet professional voice from behind me.

Immediately I cranked my head to the left to match the voice with the face. The brunette from last night.

"Bob, correct?" She held out her right hand.

I accepted her handshake, puzzled that she knew my name. "And you are?"

She released my hand, opened her tiny black purse and pulled out a business card. "Marie Moneymaker. I'm the Editor and CEO of Better Gnomes and Gardens magazine. Forgive me for my not-so formal address in this matter, but I've heard about your job situation with the local paper."

My brows flew up, uncontrollable, if I may add. "It seems that my misadventures here precede me."

Marie gave me a sharp frown, then shook her head. "Bob, I read your news article on Big Foot."

There it was the sullen sound of my heart hitting rock bottom. I'd thought that today would be a great day. Had I truly the gift of Irish Luck? Well, as it is known, the Irish didn't have the greatest of luck anyways.

"I'm sorry about that. Perhaps I shouldn't have written it and,"

"Stop that! I absolutely loved the article. The writing was no less than brilliant. Bob, you have a gift for capturing what no one else wants to talk about. I need someone of your caliber writing for my magazine. If you'll accept, the job is yours."

"Wait, let me get this straight. You're offering me a job writing for Better Gnomes and Gardens?" I paused a second to catch what air I had left in my lungs. "Where is the headquarters? Will I need to move?"

Marie let out a laugh. "The headquarters is located outside of New York. Our writers work from home constructing articles for the monthly magazine. Are you interested?"

Interested? I felt like a small child on vacation at its first theme park. I knew I had to keep my composure. Nothing good ever comes from being overly excited.

I cleared my throat, then scratched my brow. "What about compensation?"

Marie reached in her purse again, pulled out a pen, relieved me of her card and scribbled a number on the back. She tucked her pen neatly away, then looked me eye to eye and handed me the card back. "Is this figure acceptable?"

Figure? I thought maybe she had written her phone number down. I stared at the number or a long moment.

"Yes!" I exclaimed.

"Good. Call my office first thing Monday morning, and we'll get you set up." She held out her hand sideways again. "It was nice meeting you Bob, and I look forward to working with you. I'm expecting spectacular things from you."

I think I smiled, but in my shocked stupor it might not have come out that way. Marie's eyes widened for a moment, then she briskly turned and left through the front door.

"Bob! Congratulations!" Maddie called out from behind the counter.

I swerved around on the barstool, clutched tightly to the card between my fingers. "I…"

"Take a deep breath, Bob." Maddie slipped a cup of coffee in front of me before I realized my panic mode had kicked in.

I inhaled a deep breath then released it slowly. "I got a job."

Maddie giggled. "I heard. That's awesome. I knew good things would come to you, Bob. You just had to see it through."

I shook my head, looked at the card again, then shoved it in my shirt pocket. "I wouldn't have believed anything like this would happen to me. I mean, I had a dream…a big dream, Maddie. This," I patted my shirt pocket. "is more than what I'd dreamed."

"You deserve it. I'm so happy for you."

"Thank you, Maddie." I lifted the cup to my lips and tried to focus on something else before I decided to burst out in a montage of the worst kind. "So has anyone heard anything about Amelia, Finn and Lilly?"

"Oh, yes. Finn came back sometime early this morning, with Amelia and Lilly. He took care of the portal with the essence Abri collected. Amelia is at home recovering and doing better."

"How's Aubri? I know last night took a lot from her."

"Lilly is back at home with her, helping her to recover. We were all a bit worried about Aubri." Maddie sent me a warm smile as she wiped the counter in front of me. "If you hadn't convinced Doug to help, I don't know what would have happened."

I gave a chuckle, then ribbed my hand over my somewhat gruffy beard. I guess in my hurry this morning I forgot to shave. "Honestly, Charlie was the one who persuaded Doug. I just made the phone call."

Maddie pursed her lips together as her chocolate brown eyes drew into tiny slits. "Bob, if you hadn't made the phone call to Doug, he wouldn't have showed up. Trust me, Doug listens to you."

"Listens?" I laughed. "Why would he listen to me?"

"Because he likes you. Maybe Charlie did put the last hammer down, but you got through to him."

"I'm glad I could help everyone. It seemed the right thing to do. I think Doug and the fae might be able to work together. I hope they will, anyway." I took another sip, then paused. "But I thought that Faeland existed in another dimension. The time thing confuses me. How did they come back so soon?"

"You're correct about Faeland and the other dimension. Time is different there, much slower than it is here. But Finn has a gold pocket watch he uses for time travel. When they came back through the portal, he then used his pocket watch to travel back to this time. He said he would have liked to have come sooner, but it took a little longer for Amelia's treatments than he anticipated."

"Oh, well that makes sense." I sat the cup down, then peered at the specials on the black board behind Maddie. "I'm glad she's doing well. I know this little town needs her special teas."

"Yes, they do. Some Mysticals here need her more than they know. She's a great help to us all."

"I see that now. Maddie?" I began as I looked up into her warm brown eyes. "If everyone in this town is a Mystical, then if you don't mind me asking…what…" I paused, confused how I would ask her such a delicate question.

"What am I?" She arched her right brown and wiped her hands on the towel.

"Yes."

Maddie giggled, then opened her mouth, but before she could answer a customer stood abruptly from their table.

"There's been a murder at the Barksdale's!"

Did you enjoy this book?

There are more exciting characters and books to come in the Mysty Haven Mystery series!

Visit

caseycardel.com

and sign up today for all the exciting news and updates on this new paranormal series!

Casey Cardel

ABOUT THE AUTHOR

Casey Cardel lives in a small Wisconsin town where gardening, sunsets, cooking and painting are enjoyed. When not picking strawberries or tending the garden, planning the next victim in the Mysty Haven series is always on the to-do list.

For more exciting books
in the
Mysty Haven Mystery Series
Visit
caseycardel.com

Granny Grimm's Apple Pie

Ingredients

2 Deep Dish Pie Crusts

¾ cup sugar

1 teaspoon ground cinnamon

2 tablespoons butter, cut into 8 cubes

7 cups thin sliced, peeled Granny Smith apples

Directions

Preheat oven to 375 degrees F.

If using frozen pie crusts, allow them to thaw first. In one deep dish pie crust pan, layer apples. Sprinkle sugar and cinnamon on top of apples, then add butter cubes. Cover pie with 2nd pie crust, trim edges (if needed) and crimp ends to fit around the pie pan. Cut slits in the top of pie crust.

Place pie on baking sheet in oven. Bake 60 minutes or until filling is bubbly. Check pie after 30 minutes. To prevent over browning, cover pie with foil for the last fifteen minutes. Cool on wire rack.

To serve, cut a slice of pie and add a slice of extra sharp aged cheddar cheese. If pie is cold, reheat the serving in the microwave with the cheese on top. Tastes better if cheese is melted.

MENTHA PRESS

CPSIA information can be obtained
at www.ICGtesting.com
Printed in the USA
LVHW010448181022
730946LV00008B/560

9 781937 629625